Beyond the Rainbow

"Oh, Jean, I'm so frightened. What if the treatment doesn't work? What if I never get better? What if...?

Her voice faltered, a mist blurred her vision. Impatiently she dashed a hand across her eyes and glancing over at Jean she saw that her eyes were also swimming.

"Don't," said Jean shakily. "You're voicing all my fears, lying here wondering...am I really better?"

For several moments both girls allowed the tears to flow, before they wiped their eyes and gazed shamefaced at one another.

"Let's see who can sniff the loudest," Jean said with a straight face.

Kirsty emitted one of the explosive snorts that had earned her many tickings-off in the classroom.

Jean also snorted, even louder than Kirsty. Both girls stopped feeling sorry ofor themselves and this time the tears that ran down their faces were born of pure, unrestrained merriment.

BEYOND THE RAINBOW

Christine Marion Fraser

Lions
An Imprint of HarperCollins*Publishers*

First published in Great Britain in Lions in 1994
Lions is an imprint of
HarperCollins Children's Books,
a division of HarperCollins Publishers Ltd, 77-85 Fulham Palace
Road, Hammersmith, London W6 8JB
1 3 5 7 9 10 8 6 4 2

Text copyright © 1994 by Christine Marion Fraser

ISBN 0 00 674623 3

The author asserts the moral right to be identified as the author of
the work.

Printed and bound in Great Britain
by HarperCollins Manufacturing Ltd, Glasgow

PART ONE

Kirsty and Jean

Chapter 1

Kirsty awoke with a start, her pulses racing, her brow hot and moist. Flopping over on to her back she lay for a moment, wondering what it was that had wakened her so suddenly and why she had this terrible feeling of dread in the pit of her stomach.

Dreaming. Yes, that was it, she had been dreaming, it all came flooding in on her, that dream, so real, so frightening. She had been running, running, away from a great dark shadow that was able to move faster than she could. But oddly enough it never quite caught up with her though it was always just there, at her back, a shadow in the shape of an ink blob with flappy bits that looked like wings and others that were like feet, all moving and swaying and gliding forward as if to envelope her in its blackness.

And all the time she had kept on running, looking over her shoulder, trying to scream but no sound would come out.

That had been the most terrifying part, not being able to call out for help, then she had tripped and had fallen and the shadow had rushed forward and was about to pounce when she had woken up.

Kirsty shuddered, she lay quite still, trying to forget the dream, concentrating her mind on her surroundings.

The door creaked open slightly and Chanter, a big ginger cat, came boldly into the room to jump on the bed and snuggle into Kirsty, his purrs filling her ears, one eye on Snippy her hamster, who was awake in his cage on the top of her dresser. He was making little nibbling noises as he ate breakfast, his pink nose and long whiskers popping up every so often. Kirsty laughed and kissed the cat's ears. "You would just love to have poor old Snippy for breakfast, wouldn't you? Well, think again, somehow I don't think he would enjoy becoming a meal for you or any other cat."

She felt better, the spring sun was streaming through her window, making an oblong pattern on her pink carpet, its light reflecting on the walls of her room. She had chosen the wallpaper herself, pale lilac splotched with lovely big purple daisies.

"You're really not going to choose *that*, are you, Kirsty?" her mother had protested, to which Kirsty had laughed and had said she was the one who would have to live with it.

Anyway, only bits of the wallpaper showed, covered as it was with posters of her favourite pop groups.

Snippy had finished eating, he was now having a busy time running around inside his exercise wheel, watched avidly by Chanter who had temporarily abandoned washing himself.

Kirsty's eyes roved round her cosy little room: she looked at her guitar resting against the wall in the corner, at her flute lying on top of her writing table, her clothes carelessly thrown over a chair, a pair of her tights lying in a small crumpled heap on the floor.

All so normal, so reassuring . . . even so she couldn't entirely forget her dream, remnants of it remained in her mind . . . and there was still this terrible feeling of unease in her stomach . . . Then she remembered – tonight her mother was taking her to see Dr Thomson for the results of her blood tests from the local hospital.

She had been tired a lot in the last few weeks and her mother, worried about her lack of appetite and loss of weight, had marched her down to the doctor who had examined her and had decided that he wanted to arrange further investigations.

Blood tests! Kirsty shuddered at the memory. But her years of being one of the gang had made her tough. Ever since she could remember she had loved kicking a ball about and had always been eager to join the boys in a game of football.

She had made a good goalie and the boys had soon accepted her into their team. Sometimes they seemed to forget that she was a girl and never made any concessions to that fact in the rough and tumble of their games.

Occasionally it was hard going, especially when she was on the receiving end of painful knocks and bruises, the sort that made even the boys wince and go hobbling away off the field.

However, there was a distinct difference between being kicked in the shins and being stabbed in the arm with a huge syringe. That big brute of a needle had made her flinch – only slightly though – but she had bit her lip and had *made* herself look at her blood frothing into the syringe; when it was all over her father had taken her brother Andy and herself to the pictures and then to the chip shop to buy fish suppers.

Thinking about her father brought a shine to Kirsty's blue eyes. Today was Friday and tonight her father would be home from Aberdeen where he was a clerk of works for an oil company.

Every six weeks he went offshore and sometimes he flew to the main office in London when he might be away for some time. Other than that he came home every weekend to their house in Paisley and just thinking about him took some of the sting away from Kirsty's fears about visiting the doctor . . .

"Kirsty, are you awake?"

A light tap sounded on the door, it opened and Mrs McKinnon stood there, a tall fair woman with deep grey eyes, fine features and a strong, determined mouth.

"How are you today, Kirsty?" Mrs McKinnon asked.

"Fine, Mum, I'm fine," Kirsty said quickly, "don't worry so much about me."

Her eyes flashed, she hated to see the anxiety in her mother's eyes and to hear it in her voice and more than anything she resented being talked to like an ill person. Normally her mother shouted at her to get out of bed and she would keep on shouting at regular intervals till Kirsty had not only risen but had emerged from the bathroom, dressed and ready for breakfast.

"You needn't go to school today if you don't feel like it, Kirsty," Mrs McKinnon said as she took in her daughter's pale face.

"I *do* feel like it, Mum," Kirsty said with a touch of irritation. "I'm getting up, I'm getting dressed, and I'm going to school."

"Very well then, breakfast on the table in half an hour." Mrs McKinnon turned away, throwing over her shoulder as she went, "Put Chanter off the bed, Kirsty, I've told you before not to allow him up here. You know how he goes off on the tiles at night and God knows the sort of things he gets up to with other cats who might have fleas!"

This was the sort of argument that Kirsty knew and understood.

"Mum!" Kirsty raised her voice and her mother came back to stand in the doorway.

"Dad will be home tonight, won't he?"

"Yes, Kirsty, you know fine well he always comes home on a Friday so why are you asking?"

"It's just – I'm looking forward to seeing him." Kirsty's eyes flashed again, this time with happiness. She hesitated then went on quickly and abruptly, "Do you like it when Dad comes home, Mum?"

The question took Mrs McKinnon unawares. She looked embarrassed and uncertain. "Of course I do, Kirsty, what a strange thing to say. Sometimes you're like a little vixen the way you pounce on people. Why do you ask such a thing?"

Kirsty was silent for a minute as she thought about how things had changed between her parents since her father had taken the job in Aberdeen. He had done it because the money was good. For a time he had been unemployed and everything had been difficult with two growing children to feed and a hefty mortgage to pay on their spacious flat in Paisley.

There were no problems there now; in fact, things were pretty comfortable with him earning again. But he hated being separated from his family and had wanted them all to move to Aberdeen to be near him.

Mrs McKinnon, however, wouldn't hear of it. She had lived in Paisley for most of her life, all her friends were here, her social life was here, her mother was in sheltered housing a bus ride away and since she didn't keep well Mrs McKinnon

12

liked to visit her often and do what she could for her. "You'll just have to try and find another job here," Mrs McKinnon had told her husband but he had been adamant about staying on in Aberdeen.

"It's a good job and the pay is reasonable," he had argued. "You know how difficult it was when I was out of work; being employed means I can give you and the kids a decent life, I can't come back just now."

"The same thing applies to me," Mrs McKinnon had told him, "I can't leave Mother, she certainly wouldn't welcome any changes at her time of life and I'm not prepared to move away from Paisley and everything I know."

After that stalemate had existed between them. Mrs McKinnon, lonely with her husband away all week and the children at school all day, had taken a part-time job as a dentist's receptionist. She had looked happier but Kirsty had known it was only a front; on one hand she loved it when her husband came home at weekends, on the other, the niggles persisted between them.

Theirs had been a happy marriage, full of warmth and laughter, but much of that had diminished lately and Kirsty spent a lot of time thinking about it. Every married couple had their arguments, she had reasoned, Sheena O'Donal in her class swore that *her* parents argued round the clock and yet were the best of friends.

But Kirsty couldn't compare her mum and dad with the fiery O'Donals who certainly seemed to thrive on good-going verbal battles. The O'Donals didn't walk hand in hand through the park and laugh together like children as Kirsty's had done. Her parents still walked in the park but they didn't laugh nearly as much as they had and they certainly didn't hold hands any more.

Kirsty gazed at her mother standing in the doorway, waiting for her to speak. The time for questions had come, Kirsty decided, and taking a deep breath she said, "Is everything all right between you and Dad? I've heard you both arguing. And I – just wondered."

Mrs McKinnon smiled suddenly and gave her daughter an affectionate hug. "Big ears! You always did listen at doors! Dad and I are going through a bad patch. You know the reasons, he wants us all in Aberdeen, I can't leave your gran, I don't want to leave Paisley. What about you? How do you feel?"

"I don't know," Kirsty said uncertainly. "I like it here, I like my school . . . but I'm eleven now and next year I'll be leaving it anyway. Andy's feelings are a bit stronger than mine. He enjoys the grammar school, he's got lots of friends there. Both of us want Dad home full-time yet we know he might not get work here."

Mrs McKinnon sighed and said thoughtfully, "A difficult situation for us all . . . but hopefully time will resolve everything – one way or another. Get up now, Andy will want the bathroom and you know how long you take to get ready."

She went out of the room, leaving Kirsty to get slowly out of bed, her thoughts going round in furious circles. *Time will resolve everything – one way or another.*

She hadn't liked the sound of that last remark of her mother's, she hadn't liked it at all, and all that on top of everything else . . . tonight Dr Thomson's . . . the results of her blood tests.

She gulped and tried to stay calm. It would be nothing, he was just making sure, that was all. Sure about what? That she really was ill? Or making sure that she wasn't?

The questions whirled in her head. Donning her dressing-gown she went out of her room and into the bathroom, glad that she had beaten Andy to it. He was a sleepyhead in the morning and went about in a daze. When he snibbed the bathroom door that was it. She could wait for ever to get it. Brushing his teeth alone could take him ten minutes and she was certain that he sometimes fell asleep in the bath because when she listened at the door she couldn't hear him splashing about in the tub.

He was coming along the hall – like a zombie – yawning and bleary-eyed. With a giggle she shut and snibbed the bathroom door.

"Come on, Kirsty," he cried. "Don't take all day in there!"

"I'm only just in!" she called back.

There was an audible groan and his footsteps went shuffling away. She rescued a large spider from the bathtub and in minutes she was soaking herself in a froth of strawberry-scented bubbles that relaxed her and made her forget some of her anxieties.

Chapter 2

Kirsty found Andy in the kitchen, sitting at the table with his chin in his hands, gazing into space. He was still in his dressing-gown, his brown hair standing on end, his blue eyes sleepy-looking.

"What are you doing?" she asked with a smile.

He reached for a jug of fresh orange juice and poured some into a glass. "Growing old gracefully," he replied dryly, gulping down his juice, "waiting for my beard to sprout and my hair to fall out. One of these days I'm going to beat you to the bathroom and make *you* wait for a change. What do you do in there? Dismantle the plumbing and put it back together again?"

She giggled. "Och, don't be so grumpy. At least I don't fall asleep in the bath like some people I know."

She sat beside him and poured herself a glass of juice. "I spoke to Mum this morning."

"What about?"

"Her and Dad. I asked her why they niggled so much at each other."

"And?"

17

"She told me nothing we didn't know already. She wants to stay here, he wants us to move to Aberdeen."

"Ach, I wish they'd make up their minds one way or another. I hate it when they argue. The same old ground, over and over."

She gave him a long, considering look. He was fourteen, a tall lanky boy with spots on his chin and a gruff voice. They had always got on well together, sometimes he was impatient with her and called her a "kid" but mostly he was good-natured and even-tempered.

"How would you feel about moving, Andy?" she asked slowly. "Could you be happy somewhere else?"

"I like it here," he answered abruptly. "My mates are here, I like my school."

"I've always wanted to live in the country," she said dreamily, "and Aberdeenshire is lovely, all rolling fields and heathery hills."

"You're a romantic, Kirsty—" he began but was interrupted by Mrs McKinnon coming into the kitchen.

"Andy! Just look at you!" she scolded, "like something the cat dragged in! I said breakfast on the table at eight-thirty and I meant it!"

"Just going, Mum," he growled, throwing his sister a reproachful glance on his way out of the room.

It was a rush to get to school that morning. Andy

had left the soap in the sink and the hot tap dripping in the bath, Kirsty had omitted to put the top back on the toothpaste tube and she had left a sodden bathtowel on the floor.

Each had blamed the other for these small acts of carelessness but Mrs McKinnon had not been prepared to listen to their differences.

"You will *both* go and clean up the mess," she had said firmly, "and if you're late for school you'll have no one to blame but yourselves."

They knew better than to grumble, their mother was a stickler for tidiness, and they dived into the bathroom together, getting in each other's way, wasting precious time arguing about who had done what and when they had done it.

When they finally set off Kirsty was hot and breathless, Andy tousled and cross. They marched along silently, Kirsty doing her best to keep up with her brother's long stride. It was a lovely spring morning, the sun was shining, the daffodils were dancing in the gardens they passed along the way.

The sight made Kirsty feel better and after a while she confided some of her fears to Andy regarding her visit to the doctor.

"It won't be anything serious." He tried to sound reassuring though he too had been wondering about the tests. "Doctors are just people after all, they can't tell if there's anything wrong just by looking at you so they have to take blood samples."

"I was thinking about Bobby Jones; he had something wrong with his blood, he had leukaemia."

Andy stopped marching and stared at her, his eyes round. "Come on, Kirsty, don't be daft! Don't think things like that."

"I can't help it," she said miserably. "It isn't just the tests, it's why I had to have them in the first place, I *have* lost weight and I am tired a lot."

He started walking again, faster than before. "Just wait and see, don't cross bridges. Dad will be home when you get back from the doc's and we'll have a good going fireside concert after tea."

"Will you let me play your mouth-organ?"

"I might, as long as you don't blow crumbs into it."

His bluntness restored her spirits and for the rest of the way they talked of lighter things till they parted company, he going off to join a crowd of boys on their way to the Grammar, she running to catch up with a group of girls heading for the gates of the primary school.

Kirsty watched Dr Thomson's face as he leafed through some notes on his desk. She had always liked Dr Thomson, he was usually straight and to the point and didn't hum and haw like the older doctor in the practice. He was a good-looking man with kindly eyes, a straight nose, and laughter lines round his mouth.

Too bad about the pimple on his chin. Kirsty knew all about pimples. Lately she had been getting one or two on her face. Andy had teased her about them and had told her they meant she was growing up, to which she had tossed her head and had told him to go and count his *own* spots.

She wondered why was she thinking about spots at a time like this but she already knew the answer to that. It was to keep her mind off things she didn't want to think about . . . the results of those tests for instance.

Dr Thomson was frowning a bit now, really looking quite serious. Kirsty swallowed hard, she didn't like the look of that frown, it meant something in the notes wasn't pleasing him and she didn't want to know what it was. She concentrated on his pimple. It was red and angry-looking with a little yellow tip and she wondered why he couldn't cure a simple thing like a spot on his chin when he was so clever at everything else . . .

"Right, Mrs McKinnon." The doctor looked at Kirsty's mother over his specs. "I've got the report from the hospital . . ." He cleared his throat. "Those tests of Kirsty's . . . her blood count isn't quite what it ought to be. We must get her into hospital right away. I'm afraid the tests show Kirsty has leukaemia."

Hospital! Dr Thomson was definitely not

smiling when he made his pronouncement.

Kirsty's head jerked up, she stared at him, her heart beginning to thump in her throat. Surely he couldn't be talking about *her*! Other people went into places like hospital! She was Kirsty McKinnon, she had always been healthy and well. In winter, when Andy had the snuffles and sneezes she was out jogging round the block, clear-eyed and full of bounce.

"You're like a tennis ball, Kirsty," her father had once told her. "Back and forth, back and forth, never still for a minute, just watching you makes me tired."

"Hospital?" Mrs McKinnon's grey eyes were fixed on the doctor's face. Her own registered alarm and more than a touch of disbelief.

"Right away," Dr Thomson repeated, looking at Kirsty in a rather apologetic manner. "We have to see about getting you well again. You're a brave lass – and a strong one, you won't let the side down."

Kirsty was aware of a strange beating sensation in her neck, her stomach felt wobbly and weak, but she had to know more – she had always asked questions and she liked to get straight answers. "Leukaemia? Like Bobby Jones in the street next to ours whose hair fell out with the treatment he got?"

She had completely floored Dr Thomson. He stared at her over his specs and said almost without thinking, "Ay, Kirsty, like Bobby Jones – and – God, girl! You know how to pull the punches!"

Kirsty glanced quickly at her mother. She had turned pale, but for Kirsty's sake she composed herself, and taking her daughter's hand she gave it a reassuring squeeze.

Kirsty held on tightly to her mother. She didn't want to cry, not here, in the doctor's surgery . . . not in front of him.

The effort of fighting back her tears brought a lump to her throat; she felt terror rising within her, she wanted to shout and scream at the doctor, she wanted to tell him that he was mistaken, he wasn't God! He didn't know everything! None of them were gods! They had sent the wrong notes! They belonged to somebody else with a name like hers. Somebody who had . . . leukaemia . . .

Leukaemia. Leukaemia. The word whirled round in her head.

Wildly and wordlessly she stared at the doctor. Getting up he came round the desk and put a firm hand on her shoulder. "Don't be ashamed to let go, Kirsty, even brave people have to cry."

"I'll be all right," she said in a small voice. "Bobby Jones got better and so will I. I've always been strong and I'm a good fighter."

She said nothing more. All she wanted in those traumatic moments was to get outside, into the fresh air, away from the claustrophobic confines of the surgery.

She stood up. "Come on, Mum." She tried desperately to keep her voice steady. "Dad and Andy will be waiting for their tea and I'm so hungry I could eat a horse."

She wasn't in the least bit hungry, in fact she felt a little bit sick and slightly wobbly on her feet but she had to make herself strong enough to walk out of here, to get home to their nice, warm, homely home with all the familiar things around her.

Dr Thomson cleared his throat again. "Kirsty's right, Mrs McKinnon," he said with a nod, his warm, brown eyes going from mother to daughter, "she *is* a fighter. I can see that."

A glimmer of hope shone in Mrs McKinnon's eyes. "Ay, Doctor, you're right, Kirsty always was a fighter . . ." She managed a smile. "A terrible tomboy but game for anything."

"The hospital will be in touch," he told her. "Meantime you must rest as much as possible, Kirsty."

Mrs McKinnon thanked him. She put her arm round Kirsty's shoulders and they walked out of Dr Thomson's surgery into the spring sunshine.

Mother and daughter made their way in silence for a few moments, each of them pre-occupied with her own thoughts.

"Kirsty," Mrs McKinnon spoke at last, "I'm proud of the way you behaved in there. But it was so like you to want to know the truth so quickly even though it came as a great shock. I knew there was something wrong but I didn't expect – leukaemia."

"I know, neither did I, though I did think about it," Kirsty admitted. Her eyes filled up as terror welled afresh in her belly. "Mum, I can't stand it. I'm afraid, of going to hospital – but mostly I'm afraid – I might – die."

Mrs McKinnon's own eyes were moist and she searched for the right words to say. She too was afraid for her daughter's future but they would all have to be strong if they were to help her to fight her illness.

"You are very ill, Kirsty," she said frankly, knowing that it was useless trying to evade the issue. Kirsty would never stand for that, she was far too clear-sighted to be taken in by false words of comfort. "But the treatment for leukaemia has progressed a lot in recent years. Don't think about dying, just think about living, you've got all your life in front of you and you have to set your sights on that."

Kirsty took a deep breath, she pulled back her shoulders and tried to still her fears. She thought about her father and more than ever she was glad that it was Friday for, despite her show of bravery in the doctor's surgery, she very much needed her father's strong shoulder to lean on.

There was something about him that seemed indestructible. He had a great store of inner strength, he was like a rock that would never perish, no matter how old he became. Everything was better when he was home, the atmosphere was lighter and brighter and more cheerful somehow. On Friday nights even Chanter stayed in, abandoning his nocturnal pursuits in favour of a cosy snooze in front of the fire.

Suddenly Kirsty couldn't wait to see her father, she wanted to feel his strong arms around her and to hear his voice telling her that everything was going to be all right.

Chapter 3

Andy and his father received the news of Kirsty's illness in their own different ways.

Andy's eyes grew round and big in a face that was suddenly white. He gaped at Kirsty and cried protestingly, "Leukaemia! There must be a mistake! They make mistakes you know, the doctors!"

"There is no mistake, Andy," his mother said quietly. "It was all there, in Dr Thomson's notes. Kirsty has to go into hospital almost right away. The sooner she's in, the sooner she can start treatment."

"I don't believe it," he muttered. Turning on his heel he rushed away. Seconds later the door of his room shut with a bang.

Kirsty's father, a ruggedly handsome man with deep-set blue eyes, gathered her into his arms and held her long and tightly, conveying his love to her in that precious, tender way of his. "Let the tears go, Kirsty," he urged. "Bottling up your feelings won't do you any good. You have a right to cry, I would if it was me."

"I've never seen you cry," she sobbed against his shoulder.

"Well, you know what it's like, men aren't supposed to indulge in such things, something instilled in us from childhood. Just the same we *do* it. I have when I've been unhappy. It doesn't make you any less of a person. Some of the bravest people in the world have admitted to having a good old cry when faced with danger. You're my lass, I know what a staunch wee heart you've got, you needn't be afraid to show your feelings to me. I'm your dad, remember, I'll always love you and we're going to fight this thing together."

"How can you?" she said shakily. "We only ever see you at the weekends."

"I'll get time off and I'll be with you as often as I can."

"What about you and Mum? You argue with one another and Andy and I both hate it. I want it to be the way it was with you here all the time and Mum happy again. She gets so irritable with us when you're away."

"Sweetheart." He held her at arm's length and looked her straight in the eye. "I can't leave my job, it means a lot to me to be able to give my family the kind of things I couldn't give when I was out of work. I felt degraded and humiliated. Try to understand. I'll keep looking for a job here, meantime I have to stay where I am."

"But you will come and see me in hospital? I couldn't bear it if you didn't."

"Try and stop me," he said, his eyes very intense.

Over tea they discussed her illness openly and frankly, and in so doing the sting of it was somewhat eased.

"We'll look upon it as a game of football," Mr McKinnon decided and without more ado he cleared a space on the table and began to lay out a little football pitch.

"Look, Kirsty," he directed, as he arranged table accoutrement as goalposts, getting quite carried away in his enthusiasm. When he had finished, a salt-cellar represented Kirsty standing between a bottle of tomato sauce and another of malt vinegar while the pepper-pot was meant to be the opposition goalkeeper waiting between jars of beetroot and pickles. A small, pickled, silverskin onion took the role of a football and the players were an assortment of chessmen that Andy brought from his room.

"Right, Kirsty," said her father, "think of yourself out there in the playing field and get cracking saving the shots with your salt-cellar. I know that leukaemia can cause a shortage of red blood cells so we'll call the opposition the 'Lukes' while those on our side will be the 'Reds'. OK, let's go. Whistle for the start of the game, Andy."

Andy put two fingers in his mouth and gave vent to a piercing whistle and right there in the kitchen

29

a good going game of table football got underway with everyone shouting for the "Reds".

Chanter stalked into the room to see what all the fuss was about. With an agile spring he jumped up on a chair to watch the game, his head swivelling from side to side as the chessmen were pushed back and forth across the table.

Kirsty, operating her salt-cellar with great aplomb, saved one goal after another until the "Lukes" were well and truly beaten.

"Victory!" cried Mr McKinnon, throwing up his arms and waving his hands above his head.

The frivolous little interlude had taken Kirsty's mind off her troubles. With misty eyes she looked at the faces round the table. A feeling of family unity was in the air and she vowed that she would beat those "Lukes" – in the end she would beat them.

"I hope I don't lose my hair," Kirsty said to Andy when they were in his room looking out the musical instruments they would need for the family ceilidh, something that had started when they were very young and which still survived. "I know Bobby Jones lost his because of the treatment he got."

Andy gazed at her shining tresses. "Supposing you do," he said awkwardly, "it might grow back curly. You always said how much you would like to have naturally curly hair."

"But – supposing it doesn't grow back at all,"

Kirsty faltered, 'I'll be as bald as old Mr Black in the flat downstairs."

Andy didn't know how to handle such a delicate situation. The idea of his sister losing her lovely hair for ever brought home to him the reality of her illness. This morning he had teased her as usual, they had argued, they had laughed.

True, she had been worried about seeing the doctor but never in his wildest imaginings had he visualised anything being really seriously wrong with her.

Now this, taking away his sense of normality, making him look at her with new eyes, eyes that saw how thin she had become, how pale her face was . . .

He braced himself, he mustn't let her see how much this had affected him, it would only worry her if he lost his cool in front of her.

"Listen, Kirsty," he said in a voice void of emotion, "you know nothing about the treatment you'll get or how it will affect you so don't . . ."

"Cross bridges?"

"Something like that, you're always jumping to conclusions. Let's just wait and see."

"You said that this morning and look where it got me."

"Well, I wasn't to know what the hospital would say! I'm not magic and I can't read people's minds . . . Don't go on about it," he finished sullenly.

"You – won't treat me any differently, will you? I don't want people to speak to me like an ill person."

"Of course I won't treat you differently. You'll always be a wee pest – ill or no . . . and I'm fed up hearing you going on about it – so – so just shut up and take your guitar through to the living room."

Strangely enough she felt better; this was the brother she knew best. It would have been the last straw if he had looked at her with sorrow and, worse, if he had spoken to her with the pitying tones of a stranger.

With Kirsty and Andy out of the room Mrs McKinnon had a chance to talk to her husband. "You will try to get home more?" she asked. "This has been a great shock to Kirsty, she'll need you now more than ever before."

"And you, Jan, will you need me?"

She glanced at him quickly. "You know I can't leave Paisley. I want to be near you, but I can't leave Mother, and with Kirsty going into hospital there's more need than ever to stay here. I'm afraid, Bob, more afraid than I've ever been in my life."

"I too am afraid. I never thought it would come to this, our wee lass, so ill, you and me like strangers. But I can't leave my job, Jan. If it's your mother you're worried about we can soon solve that. We could buy a house big enough for her to live with us. We might even be lucky enough to get one with a granny flat. Why don't you ask her?"

"All right, I will," she agreed. "Though you know how independent she is and will likely turn up her nose at anything I have to say."

The very next day she went to visit her mother, telling her first about Kirsty's illness. Granny Reid, as she was known to the children, was shocked.

"Kirsty? As ill as that! Och, my poor wee bairn, you must all be worried sick about her."

"We are, Mother, it was so unexpected, but you know Kirsty, she's being very brave about it though I know that, deep down, she's dreading going into hospital."

They spoke about Kirsty for a long time then Mrs McKinnon brought up the subject of moving to Aberdeen.

"Aberdeen?" Granny Reid's voice fell an octave. "I don't think so, Jan. I'm as settled here as I'll ever be." She was a strong-featured, determined-looking woman, full of life and an indomitable spirit which made her popular with her grandchildren. Nothing floored Granny Reid, not even the heart condition from which she suffered. She led a full and active life and always entered into the spirit of anything that was going on.

"I thought you'd say that," said Jan McKinnon

despairingly. "You've made a niche here, you have your friends and all the things you know round about you."

"Och, you mustn't stay because of me," Granny Reid was immediately on the defensive.

"Mother, I'm your daughter, I have to be near at hand in case you need me, that's the reason I'm asking you these things." Suddenly Granny Reid's face brightened. "Och, Jan, I've just thought of Red Rowans, the family home in Donside, all closed up since your Aunt Bella died. I've thought about it so often, the fun we had there as children, me and Bella. Oh, ay, I wouldn't mind moving if it was to Red Rowans. I've known it all my life."

"No, Mother," her daughter said firmly, "not to Red Rowans, it must be falling apart by now. It's too difficult to look after an old house like that. I meant to another house entirely."

"Jan, have you thought about the children. What they would like?"

"Mother! Of course I've thought about them! Andy is quite happy in Paisley, Kirsty has never expressed any strong opinions about staying or leaving so she must be contented enough."

"Ay, but I know my wee lass, she keeps a lot of her feelings hidden. When I speak about Red Rowans her face lights up. Poor wee lass,' Granny Reid shook her head, "I can't really believe she's so ill. She looked thin and pale the last time I saw her but I never dreamed she had leukaemia. Tell her I'll come and see her in hospital."

"She'll be delighted to see you. I'll come and fetch you and we'll go together."

"I can manage on my own."

"It would be better if I was there, the infirmary is quite far away."

"Och, all right, have it your way. You always do."

Her daughter saw an argument coming on so she collected her things and hastily left.

"Well, what did she say?" Bob McKinnon asked as soon as his wife got home.

"Determined as usual. She doesn't want to move unless it's to Red Rowans."

His face lit up. "Red Rowans! I never thought of that. I love that old house. What could be more perfect? Big enough for us all. No need to buy a newer house that might cost a fortune."

"No, Bob, not Red Rowans, the place must be practically a ruin by now. It would be false economy. *It* would cost a fortune to modernise . . ." Fondly she glanced round the room, everything up to date, all of it clean and easy to run. "I'm certainly not leaving here to go to a dark and dismal Victorian mansion and Mother won't come with us to what she calls a strange house . . ."

"So, we're back to where we started?"

"If you want to put it that way – yes."

Bob McKinnon's jaw tightened and one word borrowed another. When Kirsty came into the room and heard her parents arguing she gave vent to a long sigh as she wondered when and how the problems were going to resolve themselves . . . if ever.

Chapter 4

A few days later Kirsty was admitted to hospital, a big, daunting and unreal place. So Kirsty thought as she lay in the unfamiliar bed, listening to all the strange sounds, watching the activities of the nurses.

It seemed ages since her parents had brought her up to the ward. They hadn't been able to stay long because the doctor had wanted to see them to explain about the treatment she would be getting. That had been half an hour ago but to Kirsty it was like eternity.

She felt terribly alone, home was already another world away. Andy would be in school, her friends would be talking about her being in hospital, they would be sympathetic but would breathe signs of relief that it was she and not they who was ill.

She slid down in the starched bed, as if by so doing she would be less conspicuous and could be alone for a while with her thoughts.

How long would she be here, she wondered. Days? A week perhaps? She couldn't bear to be cooped up any longer than that. The doctor had said he would come and talk to her when she was settled. When she was settled! As if she ever would be. She had never felt more miserable, more lonely. All she wanted was to be back home, feeling that she was one of the gang, kicking a ball about in that lovely wide playing field with the sky and the trees all around.

Freedom! She longed for that more than anything. She had always loved the outdoors, her one great desire was to one day live in the country where buzzards soared in the sky and the deer came down from the hills in winter, just as they had done when she and her family had spent some wonderful Christmas holidays with Great-aunt Bella in Red Rowans, in the north of Scotland.

Great-aunt Bella had been quite ancient, with snow-white hair and a big purple nose that always looked cold, no matter how warm the fire or how stuffy the room. Her lively blue eyes had twinkled a lot and she had told marvellous stories about her girlhood days when she had been a maidservant in one of the big gentry houses in Braemar.

Her descriptions of life in the big house had been vivid and colourful. She'd had to rise very early to light fires and take morning tea to the members of the household. One of these had been an old titled gentleman whose habit of wearing a tassled nightcap in bed had amused her greatly. He had taken her into his confidence regarding his liking for whisky in his tea – "Or was it tea in his whisky?" Great-aunt Bella would say with a mischievous chuckle.

This same gentleman had been a naughty but harmless old devil with the ladies as the young Bella had found out one morning when he had tried to give her a playful squeeze. She had reacted with typical good humour. "Sir," she had said with a straight face, "you really mustn't do that, ever since I can remember I've been a very tickly sort o' person, I just scream and scream and bring everyone running to see what's wrong with me. You, sir, with your good reputation to uphold, wouldn't like that, would you now?"

Her work in the big house had been very, very hard but she had enjoyed herself too and had spoken with affection of the dances the gentry had arranged for the servants and of the ceilidhs and bothy nights she had attended in the local village hall.

Great-aunt Bella had been Granny Reid's older sister and when the two of them got together they had reminisced about their childhood days spent at Red Rowans, talking about the village school they had attended, their walks in the hills when the heather was in bloom, picnics with their parents on the banks of the River Don, the marvellous old characters who had made their childhood memorable and special.

But Great-aunt Bella was gone now, having

died two years ago. Red Rowans was boarded up and deserted and there were no more lovely holidays in magical Donside.

Kirsty lay back on her pillows, remembering those times in the country with Andy and her parents and sometimes Granny Reid, the snowball fights they'd had, all of them laughing and slithering about in the snow and pelting one another with big, fat, powdery snowballs, while Granny Reid and her sister looked on, smiling, perhaps remembering days when they too had played in the snow.

Kirsty's parents had been happier with each other in those days, full of fun and laughter and often seeming like children themselves in their eagerness for life. She gazed unseeingly into space, thinking about them as they were now, neither of them giving in to the other. She could understand her father wanting to hold on to his job; he had been utterly dejected when he had been out of work and had grown quiet and withdrawn. He was more like his old self again – up to a point – and that point came when he and her mother started arguing . . .

A cold sensation of dread washed over her. What if they drifted apart and the family split up? She didn't know how she could cope with that. She loved that big, handsome Dad of a man, she loved her mother . . .

A lump came to her throat. She knew that any moment now she was going to dive under the sheets to howl her eyes out and make a terrible fool of herself in front of all those strange people in the ward . . .

"Hallo, when did you get in? I was asleep and didn't hear anything."

The girl in the next bed to Kirsty propped herself up on one elbow and gave the newcomer a friendly smile. "Don't look so alarmed, you'll soon get used to all the commotion. My name's Jean Anderson, I'm eleven and I've been here for two weeks. I've had an operation for a lump in my knee. It was cancer and at first the doctors thought I would have to lose my leg. Then they decided it wasn't bad enough for that so they took the lump away instead."

Kirsty tried to absorb all of this. She noticed the cage round Jean's legs, the bedclothes made it look like a covered wagon in a western movie. Jean herself had long fair hair and laughing green eyes. Kirsty liked the look of her; she also liked Jean's lilting voice and the friendliness of her manner.

Kirsty told Jean her name, then she said quickly, "I've got something wrong with my blood, leukaemia. I hate it, I hate being here, I don't want it, I don't want to be ill!"

"Do any of us?" Jean said heavily. "You don't think we're all here for the good of our health, surely."

Kirsty had to smile at this. She didn't feel so alone now and she felt herself warming towards

41

Jean. She found herself wanting to know more about her new-found friend and the questions came tumbling out.

"I'm from an island in the Hebrides called Sanda." Jean was only too happy to talk about her family. "I live with my parents and two brothers on a croft near the beach, Rob is fourteen and Jim is thirteen and they're both a pair of tearaways."

She glanced affectionately at a photograph on her bedside cabinet. "That's them there, faces clean for a change. Rob's a great help to Dad on the croft and Jim just mucks in on anything that's going."

Kirsty looked at the photo of two boys, Rob with dark hair and brown eyes, Jim fair-haired and carefree-looking.

"They and my parents come and visit me whenever they can," Jean went on. "It's difficult with them being so far away but it's a school holiday soon and the boys are coming to stay with an aunt in Glasgow so I'll see a lot more of them."

Kirsty loved the way that Jean pronounced "Glasgow" in her clear musical voice.

"Can you speak the Gaelic?" she enquired.

"Yes, we're all taught it in school and of course it's my parents' native tongue." Clearing her throat she opened up with a few Gaelic expressions: "*Kemmer a ha oo*. That means 'how are you?' And you say, '*Ha me goo ma*', I am well."

Kirsty giggled as she tried out the strange words. "It's a lovely language," she said sincerely, "so lilting and romantic. Is it difficult to learn?"

"Some people find it hard, but if you really want to try it I'll teach you, it will help to pass the time. With a name like McKinnon you're bound to have connections with an island clan."

"You're right," said a delighted Kirsty. "My great-grandfather came from Barra to work in Paisley a long, long time ago, and our family have lived in Paisley ever since."

"Cup of tea, girls?"

A cheery voice broke into the conversation and a pink smiling face beamed upon Kirsty. "I'm Nurse Bradley. If there's anything you need just call me, meantime, here's a biscuit to go with your tea." She placed two steaming mugs beside the girls and moved on up the ward, calling out cheerful greetings to the occupant of each bed.

"I dreaded coming into hospital," Kirsty admitted to Jean as she sipped her tea and munched her biscuit. "I don't feel so bad now – for the moment at least. Meeting you has certainly helped."

Jean grinned. "You might not say that once you get to know me. I've got a temper – with two brothers I have to be able to stick up for myself."

"I've got a brother." Kirsty couldn't keep a note of pride from her voice. "His name's Andy, he's fourteen and he plays the flute in the school orchestra. He's tall and gangly and a bit grumpy at times but we manage to get along with one another. I'm learning to play the guitar and the flute and we practise together as often as we can."

"That sounds terrific," said Jean enthusiastically. "My family are all musical, my dad plays the accordion, Mum plays the fiddle, I do a bit of singing and play the spoons and Rob and Jim are both learning the bagpipes. We have great ceilidh nights on the island and sometimes we have sausage sizzles and sing songs on the beach and go swimming in the sea if it's warm enough."

Kirsty was uplifted by Jean's merry chatter and felt as if she had been transported to Sanda with its music and its beaches and its great seas crashing to the shore. She lay back on her pillows, grateful to Jean for having taken away some of her homesickness. Even so, it seemed a long time to go till visiting; she was longing to see her father's handsome, strong face, and to feel her mother's hand curling into hers. Andy might bring his mouth-organ so that she could play it quietly and help fill up the long hours in bed.

"Jean," she said suddenly, "weren't you afraid when you thought you might have to lose your leg?"

"Terrified. It's been with me a long time and I've got used to having it. Seriously, I felt sick at the idea. I got really depressed and was a bitch

44

to live with. Nobody could get through to me, I wouldn't let them; then the doctors decided to let me keep it and I can't tell you how relieved I was. Mind you, I still had to go through an operation to have the lump removed. It's gone now though and the doctors are optimistic that the cancer's gone too. I'm getting chemotherapy treatment as a precaution against further tumours. It makes me feel queasy. And my hair is thinning down a bit, but it's a lot better than losing my leg."

Kirsty gazed at Jean's shining tresses and she swallowed hard. "That's what I'm afraid of – getting the sort of treatment that might make me – lose my hair."

"Och, don't worry," Jean said comfortingly. "It might never come to that – and even if it does, it'll grow back in, maybe thicker than before. Nobody likes to part with bits of their bodies but hair at least can come back – not like a leg – or an arm – or even an eye – so your hair should be the least of your problems at the moment."

Kirsty was silent for a few minutes, then she reached out with her hand to Jean and said with feeling, "I'm glad to have met you, Jean Anderson."

"Me too – you," Jean said and smiled, a slow, radiant smile that was like a tonic in itself.

Kirsty was aware of weariness creeping up on her; her eyelids were like lead, her eyelashes fluttered to her cheeks. Tired but glad, so glad that she had been fortunate enough to land up beside Jean Anderson, a girl she felt she had known all her life even though they had met just a short time ago.

Chapter 5

Kirsty saw Dr Kominski for the first time when she awoke from her sleep. He was standing at her bedside, a tall man with fair hair, brown eyes and a little pointed beard. His brow was furrowed, his mouth unsmiling, and Kirsty thought he seemed rather forbidding as he stood there looking down on her.

"Hallo, I'm Dr Kominski," he introduced himself. Kirsty noticed that his beard wiggled up and down as he spoke. "I'm here to look after you but I'm not doing a very good job, am I? Waking you up from that lovely deep sleep you were in."

His smile removed the grimness from his face but even so she felt slightly awed by him. She had heard stories about doctors who thought they were gods and who went strutting about, dishing out orders in loud booming voices and expecting everyone to rush to their bidding.

She remembered the things that Mary Blair had said about *her* hospital experiences. Mary Blair was two classes below Kirsty in school. Since coming to Paisley a year ago Mary had taken a liking to Kirsty and had confided a lot in her.

Mary was small and fair and prone to terrible giggling fits but she hadn't giggled nearly so much since she'd had an emergency operation for her appendix. In fact she had been positively subdued for quite some time and when Kirsty had asked her what was wrong she had recounted the first of her Dr Ogre tales. According to Mary, Dr Ogre had been ugly and bald with bulging eyes and waxy skin and "the most horrible blood-red lips you ever saw".

"Everyone said he reminded them of a vampire," Mary had gone on, her eyes big and black as she spoke. "He was the one who removed my appendix and ever since then I haven't felt well . . . as if all the blood had been sucked from my veins and replaced with water . . ."

Kirsty had smiled at Mary's stories – but that was before she herself had landed up in hospital, in a ward that reeked of antiseptic, surrounded by people who were so ill they couldn't seem to open their eyes but just lay as if they were already dead and buried.

All of this had added to Kirsty's worries and fears, making her feel vulnerable and ready to believe that there might be some grain of truth in Mary's stories.

"I hope you're feeling more at ease now, Kirsty," Dr Kominski said as he examined her. "And of course, you'll soon settle in with Jean beside you."

Kirsty was immediately ashamed of all her weird thoughts. At his kindly words she flushed a little and vowed not to be influenced by what she had heard of doctors and hospitals. He straightened and she said with typical candour, "Doctor, I know I've got leukaemia and I was wondering . . . could you tell me please . . . how do you treat it? And what exactly is it anyway?"

He took her hand and held it firmly. "Earlier on, I spoke to your parents and explained about your illness and its treatment, so now it's your turn. Somewhere in the bone marrow the genetic make-up of a single cell changes, it's as if it goes haywire, multiplies, turns leukaemic and starts to crowd out the normal cells till a sort of invasion takes place inside the body. It's up to us to fight the abnormal cells with drugs and that's what we'll be doing with you – so prepare yourself for battle, young lady. We can do our part but you must do yours as well. A fighting spirit will go a long way to helping you get well again."

Kirsty squeezed his hand, harder than she meant, and he gave a murmur of protest. She apologised, explaining that she did the same sort of thing to her brother when they were trying to prove their strength to one another. She needn't have worried; the doctor just laughed and told her she was stronger than she looked. "A good thing too, Kirsty. I can see that nothing is going to keep *you* pinned to your bed."

"I'll do my best, Doctor, even though it's all a bit scary and horrible."

"Good girl, that's what I like to hear." He placed his stethoscope back in his pocket and made a few notes for the ward sister. "Your treatment will start right away, Kirsty: antibiotics combined with some chemotherapy. Everyone reacts differently to these drugs; you might feel a bit sick and not up to the mark, only time will tell."

"How long will I be in here? And what about – my hair?"

He glanced at her mane of glossy brown hair. "Your pride and joy, eh? Well, I have to be frank, some of it might come out. If it does you mustn't worry, it will come back given time. As for the length of your stay here, that depends on how well you respond to treatment. Don't worry, we won't keep you in any longer than we have to. Meanwhile you won't have to stay in bed *all* the time, just for a day or two till you feel better. I'll be back to see how you're progressing."

He smiled at her and moved on, chatting to all the patients in turn, a tall, white-coated figure, his manner reassuring, his hands firm but gentle.

"I'm glad I'll be able to get up soon," Kirsty said to Jean. "How about you?"

"Tomorrow, just to the bathroom to begin with. I can't wait, I hate lying here when there's so much to do outside. I can't remember a time

50

when I had so little to do and so much time to do it in. I'll be stuck in here for at least another fortnight because of the treatment I'm getting."

"Och, come on, it's not so bad," Kirsty tried to sound as if she really meant it, despite a tide of homesickness that came rushing in on her. "We have each other and we'll fill our time somehow. Perhaps we could ask for our beds to be pushed together so that we can do jigsaws and play cards. I know lots of games. I play them with Andy . . . and, oh, Jean, I'm so frightened. What if the treatment doesn't work? What if I never get better? What if . . .?" Her voice faltered, a mist blurred her vision, she swallowed hard and only just managed to stop herself bursting into tears. Impatiently she dashed a hand across her eyes and glancing over at Jean she saw that her eyes were also swimming.

"Don't," Jean said shakily. "You're voicing everything that I've been thinking since my op, lying here wondering . . . am I really better? Has the cancer gone completely? Will I get more tumours somewhere else in my body? If so will it go on and on till the doctor's can't cure me any more? Will I . . . die?"

Jean's tears spilled over, and before you could say "blink" both girls were giving vent to what Jean's dad would have called "a good greet".

For several moments they allowed their emotions full rein before they wiped their eyes and gazed shamefaced at one another.

51

"Let's see who can sniff the loudest," Jean said with a straight face.

Kirsty emitted one of the explosive snorts that had earned her many a ticking-off in the classroom. Jean also snorted, one that was even louder than Kirsty's. Both girls stopped feeling sorry for themselves and in two seconds flat they were rolling about in their beds and this time the tears that ran down their faces were born of pure, silly, unrestrained merriment.

Chapter 6

That evening, when the time came for visiting, Andy was the first in the ward. As he rushed up to Kirsty's bed with gangly steps he stumbled and dropped the bag of fruit he had been carrying. Kirsty and Jean started to giggle as the apples, oranges and pears rolled all over the floor and under the beds.

Andy, his face as red as a beetroot, was more than a little relieved when Nurse Bradley came up the ward, looking calm, cool and collected.

"Ach, don't fuss," she told him while she helped him pick up the fruit. "I'll soon have it washed and fit to eat. You go and say hallo to your sister. She's been waiting to see you all day."

By this time the ward was full of visitors with their bunches of flowers and bags of sweets. A hum of voices filled the air.

"Hallo, Kirsty." Andy's greeting to his sister was offhand. His parents had told him all about the talk they'd had with Dr Kominski and at last Andy had faced the truth about Kirsty's illness. Ever since the results of her blood tests he hadn't wanted to acknowledge the fact that his sister was so seriously ill. Now he had to: she was in hospital to prove it. She looked white and drawn and so unlike the vivacious girl he had grown up with, he felt sick with dread but was determined not to show it.

"How do you feel?" he went on, still in that same nonchalant tone.

"Better now you're here. That was a great entrance."

"Och, let it drop," he growled, still smarting from embarrassment.

Kirsty tried to keep a straight face. "Best to leave the dropping to you, grumpy. Cheer up, none of us is perfect. I want you to meet somebody, Jean Anderson. She's the same age as me and comes from an island called Sanda in the Hebrides."

Jean flashed Andy a mischievous smile. "Is this the big, handsome brother you've been telling me about, Kirsty? Pleased to meet you, Andy. I like boys with a bit of flair." Jean knew how to tease, she was always doing it to her brothers though on this occasion her quick smile took the edge away from her words.

Andy nodded to Jean and muttered abruptly, "Hi, Jean, been here long?"

"A fortnight."

"Too bad. Your leg?"

"Ay, it was a tumour, I've had it removed."

"Oh."

"Don't look like that. It won't bite – my leg I mean."

"Sorry." Andy was nonplussed. He turned

hastily back to his sister, putting a hand to his face in an attempt to hide the blush on his cheeks.

"Have you been practising your flute for the orchestra?" Kirsty asked, eager to hear all the news.

"You make it sound as if you've been away for ever. You only came here this morning, remember, and I've only had one practice since then." He was unwilling to expand further. The school concert was taking place the following week and as it seemed unlikely that Kirsty would be there the thought depressed him greatly.

Kirsty was surprised at his reticence. Normally he bubbled with enthusiasm when discussing music. She hoped he wasn't going to start treating her like an ill person and was about to open her mouth to tell him so when she saw her parents coming up the ward with Granny Reid.

"Gran!" Kirsty was delighted to see the old lady. "I'm really pleased you could come. Did you make it on your own?"

"No, your mother insisted on coming to get me." Granny Reid threw her daughter a reproachful glance. "She doesn't think I'm capable of doing anything by myself."

Kirsty laughed and hugged her gran. "Och, don't be silly, I know you can do lots by yourself and so does Mum. She just likes to look after you – and it's easy to get mixed up with what bus you should take. I've often boarded the wrong one by mistake."

"We met Dad and Andy at the hospital gates," explained Mrs McKinnon, bending to give Kirsty a kiss on her cheek.

"I brought you some fruit." Granny Reid dumped a lumpy brown-paper bag on the bed filled to the brim with oranges.

"Oh, Gran," Kirsty said with a laugh. "if I go on this way I'll be able to set up a fruit stall right here in the middle of the ward!" She gazed at the familiar faces surrounding her. "It's great to see you all. I felt really lost when I came in this morning but Jean helped me get over some of it."

They were introduced to Jean before sitting themselves round Kirsty's bed to discuss with her what the doctor had said about the treatment she would be getting.

"Dr Kominski's a good man, sweetheart,' said Mr McKinnon. "He sounded very hopeful about your progress."

"Look, Kirsty, I brought your favourite goonie." Mrs McKinnon pulled Kirsty's dressing-gown from her bag. "It will help make you feel at home." Kirsty bit her lip. The sight of such a well-loved garment brought the tears to her eyes and for a few awkward moments she simply couldn't bring herself to speak.

"Next time I come I'll bring your little stereo and all your favourite tapes." Andy rushed to his sister's rescue. "And I brought you my mouth-organ so that you can play it to yourself when you get lonely. All your classmates are asking for you, also Mary Blair who says she'll be coming to see you as soon as she can. Oh, and Miss Mitchell, your PT teacher, gave me this to give to you." From his pocket he extracted a little crystal pendant in the shape of a pear drop. "She sent it with her love and said she hoped you would soon be well and strong again."

Kirsty took the pendant and holding it in her hand she stared at it, amazed to think that Miss Mitchell, who was big and manly with a booming voice and a terrible taskmaster in the gym, should remember her in this way. Miss Mitchell couldn't understand anyone who either couldn't or wouldn't show the same sort of enthusiasm for athletics that she had and she would go quite red in the face and sweat a bit at the sight of some poor exhausted girl struggling away on the bars. "You're not trying, girl!" she would bellow. "Get those muscles working or you'll be a weakling for the rest of your life!"

Miss Mitchell was a keen archaeologist and frequently went off on weekend explorations with members of a local society. She also went abroad every year to poke and dig joyfully into ancient sites of interest, and she always returned fired with enthusiasm and full of talk about her adventures, details of which she poured into any available ear, willing or otherwise.

Kirsty had never credited her with any sort of normal sensitivity, now here was this little crystal, nestling in her hand, making her realise that even hard-hearted beings like Miss Mitchell had a soft and caring side to their nature.

When the bell went for the end of visiting it seemed like a death-knell in Kirsty's ears. Andy had moved over to Jean's bed to chat with her and he had become totally entranced with her gaiety and her descriptions of her life back home on the island of Sanda.

"Do you like her?" Kirsty whispered, a sprite of mischief dancing in her eyes.

Andy's ears reddened. "She's got sense," he admitted. "Not silly and empty-headed like some girls." His eyes lit up. "Her talk of that island of hers was exciting. I could almost hear the sea booming and the gulls screeching."

"Take care, sweetheart." Mr McKinnon bent to give his daughter a kiss. "I'll be in to see you as often as I can. I'm taking some leave that's due me so you'll be seeing quite a lot of me for a while."

Kirsty gazed at him and whispered, "You and Mum . . . is everything all right?"

"Och, lassie, don't worry about us," he chided gently. "You're the important one at the moment and you must get better. The house is dead without you."

"Mum, take care of Dad." Kirsty murmured the words into her mother's ear when she was saying her goodbyes.

Mrs McKinnon's grey eyes looked misty for a moment. Straightening she said softly, "Of course I will, Kirsty, you say such strange things sometimes. I'll take care of you all, and you especially. I miss you in the house and both Snippy and Chanter are lost without you."

"Bye, sis." Andy dropped a hasty kiss on her cheek. "I'll see you."

Granny Reid was the last to leave. Gathering her granddaughter into her arms she held her for a long time and Kirsty never wanted to let go of her. "Goodbye, my dear wee lass," whispered the old lady. "I'll pray for you, I'll be thinking about you and I'll be back to see you soon."

"Bye, Gran," Kirsty said in a muffled voice.

They all moved off, and Kirsty waved at them till she could see them no more. In minutes the hitherto crowded ward was silent again and had about it that air of sober contemplation that comes after happy exhilaration.

Kirsty lay back on her pillows, feeling devastated and alone. The pangs of dread were with her again, combined with a terrible sensation of having been abandoned by her own family. They could all go away, back into the real world, and she had to stay here, separated from them because of this hateful illness that had turned everything upside-down. For quite some minutes she felt very sorry for herself until she glanced over at Jean and saw how lonely she looked with her head turned away and her eyes gazing unseeingly out of the window.

Kirsty was all at once ashamed and angry at herself. She had been surrounded by visitors while Jean had had no one to share her innermost thoughts and feelings.

"Look, Jean," Kirsty said, holding up her dressing-gown. "Do you like my goonie? My Uncle Sammy brought it back from China, he's in the Merchant Navy and travels all over the world. Just look at it, Jean, each pattern has a story to tell."

She pointed out Chinese girls helping in the kitchen and in the fields, doing their lessons in school, working with the fishing nets, playing musical instruments, dancing, taking part in all kinds of sport. "It's so colourful," Kirsty said fondly, "and it always puts me in a good mood whenever I wear it."

"It reminds me of my island life back home on Sanda." Jean spoke with a dreamy voice. "The shell-sand beaches, the blue-green water, the rocky coves, the fishermen setting out in the sunset, their boats a dark silhouette against the honey-gold sky . . ."

Kirsty held her breath. Jean's descriptions of her island were so vivid they seemed to bring a mosaic of colour and life right into the hospital ward. Kirsty was aware that there was something very special about this girl from the western isles; Jean was filled with the wonder and beauty of life and she knew how to put her feelings into words.

"There are one or two small islands just a

stone's throw from Sanda's south end," Jean went on, speaking in a far-away voice, as if she lay no more in her hospital bed but had been transported back to Sanda's well-loved shores. "They're called the Freshnish Isles. Rob and Jim and me sometimes row across in the dinghy to spend a day on them. On the biggest island, there are two caves and when it's high tide you can row the boat right inside. It doesn't matter which way the wind is coming because one cave is facing east, the other west, so one of them is always sheltered."

Kirsty listened entranced as Jean went on to tell of youthful adventures on the Freshnish Isles when she and her brothers had played pirates and had cooked shellfish on hot stones round their driftwood fire while Rob told them stories of mermaids and sea witches and horrible hags that rose up out of the waves to grab the unwary fishermen from their boats.

Kirsty shivered with delight. "You make it sound so wonderful, I'd love to visit Sanda for myself one day but I suppose we'll have to get better first."

"Yes, we'll have to get better first."

Jean still spoke in her far-away voice as she stared out of the window at the grey clouds scudding across the sky, as free and effortlessly as the gulls that rode the air thermals in Sanda's wide and endless heavens.

61

Chapter 7

The arrival of old Meg Munroe into the ward caused a terrible upheaval. Although she was small and frail her eyes were bird-bright and she really seemed to enjoy having the nurses scurrying to her bidding.

Straight away she grumbled about the position of her bed. It was too near the window, she said, the sun hurt her eyes and made her too hot. Combined with all that, the long radiator under the window was making her temperature shoot up to boiling point, and in her state of health she was simply too weak to be able to withstand that sort of thing.

She was no sooner in bed but she was calling for a bedpan. When it came she sat enthroned upon it for fully fifteen minutes and produced nothing. As soon as it was taken away she repeated the order, keeping her finger pressed on her bedside buzzer till its demands brought a probationer nurse puffing hastily up the ward.

"If I don't get a bedpan *at once*, I will wet the bed," she sternly told the little junior nurse whose pleasant rosy face was rosier still from all her rushing.

In two minutes flat the bedpan arrived under its discreet green paper covering but by that time old Meg decided that she didn't need it after all and ordered that it was to be taken away at once. But old Meg was no longer dealing with little Nurse Osborne who had been urgently called to some other menial task. This time the bearer of the bedpan was large and hefty Nurse McLeod who hailed from the island of Harris and who had carried creels of peat from an early age.

Nurse McLeod's strength was legendary. When she had worked in the men's ward it was said that she had ruled with a rod of iron and woe betide any mere mortal male who had ever tried to get the better of her. Nurse McLeod was therefore "just the boy" to put old Meg Munroe in her place as that lady found out for herself when the screens were whipped round her bed.

Wearing a very grim expression indeed, Nurse McLeod tossed back the bedcovers, lifted the old lady up as if she were a feather and dumped her unceremoniously down on the bedpan.

"Mrs Munroe," said Nurse McLeod firmly, "you will sit on that bedpan and you will stay on it till you use it and I will be back in five minutes to make sure that you have."

She emerged from the screens to stump away down the ward, leaving old Meg speechless for once in her life.

This little drama was much to the satisfaction of Miss Alice Kennedy whose drooping jowls and baggy eyes gave her the appearance of a sorrowful bloodhound.

At seventy-two years of age, Alice had been the most senior inmate of the ward . . . until the arrival of Meg Munroe that is. Meg was eighty if she was a day, and old Alice wasn't at all pleased to see her, in fact she was positively disgruntled by all the fuss and upsets, and was cheered considerably by Nurse McLeod's tough handling of the aged troublemaker.

Despite Nurse McLeod, Meg got her way over the position of her bed. When Nurse McLeod went off duty the old lady listed her complaints directly to the ward sister with the result that her bed, her belongings and herself were moved to a more central position in the ward.

Miss Alice Kennedy's nostrils flared with indignation as she lay witnessing this latest manoeuvre and she didn't mince words when she said in a loud voice for everyone to hear, "*Some* people just like to bring attention upon themselves! As if the nurses weren't busy enough without having extra burdens put upon them. I was brought up to believe that it was the height of bad manners to make a spectacle of oneself."

Old Alice was putting on her most snobbish voice. Her father had been a Church of Scotland minister and his children had been brought up in the rather genteel confines of the church manse.

They had been expected to attend regular Sunday worship and to behave themselves in public places and had been taught never, never, to discredit either the Church or the family by loud and brash behaviour.

A devilish grin lit Meg's old face as the words of Miss Alice Kennedy fell upon her ears. "Ay, that's why you'll be such a girning rascal now," she intoned in a voice as loud, if not louder, than that of her new-found rival. "Too many restrictions in anyone's life can turn them into sour and dried-up busybodies with all their emotions suppressed inside themselves. You'll likely be a spinster woman, I've no doubt of that, you've got that look of discontent on your face that only a good man and a few bairns would have cured."

The truth of this was almost too much for Miss Alice Kennedy. She choked on a mint imperial she had been sucking and it was only through the timely arrival of Nurse Bradley that she was able to recover both her equilibrium and her breath.

The new positioning of Meg's bed meant that she was now almost directly opposite Kirsty and Jean. Both girls were utterly fascinated by the ancient tearaway. Her noisy arrival had roused them from the state of lethargy into which they had sunk in the past few days. Kirsty's treatment had made her tired and listless. Jean's leg had been giving her a lot of pain and she had lost much of the sparkle that she had tried so hard to maintain since the start of her illness. With everyone else in the ward intent on their own troubles there was little to stimulate the spirits of two young girls. Meg was just the tonic they needed to lift them out of themselves.

Their interest in her was further strengthened when, later that afternoon, two round hard objects came whizzing across the ward like little golf balls, one to land in Jean's lap, the other to go bouncing off Kirsty's bed and on to the floor.

At first they thought they were being bombarded by hostile objects and instinctively dived under the blankets but when Kirsty eventually peeped over the edge of the blanket she laughed when she saw a black striped ball lying innocently on the floor.

With a giggle she hopped out of bed to pick up the sweet and popped it into her mouth, and Jean, realising that she wasn't under siege, did exactly the same as her friend.

"Thank you, Mrs Munroe," they called in unison.

"Call me Meg, Mrs Munroe is too formal for an old troublemaker like me." As she spoke she slid Miss Alice Kennedy a twinkling sidelong glance which made that lady snort "Hmph!" in a most unladylike manner and huffily hunch her shoulders in a definitely unsociable gesture.

Having had the satisfaction of once more ruffling Miss Kennedy's feathers, Meg turned her attention back to the girls. "You're smiling, that's the spirit. As my old mother used to say:

'Keep smiling though the skies are grey,
And look upon the bright side.
But if no bright side you can see,
Then polish up the dark side.

'Never cry when you can laugh,
Keep your spirit soaring free,
Let the battle cry ring forth.
We truly are for ever going to be!' "

"These are lovely words, Meg. Is it a song?" Kirsty asked.

"No, just a wee verse, but maybe you could put a tune to it. I remember my brothers and sisters used to make up tunes and poems when we were all young together back home in Greenock and my mother would give a small prize for the best tune. It was a great game and we were so happy then. The boys were all killed in the war and my sisters died, one after the other. I'm the only one left out of a family of seven but I've had a good life and I've no regrets."

The words of Meg's verse were racing through Kirsty's head. She began to hum a simple tune which was quickly taken up by Jean and then by Meg in her quavery but tuneful voice.

Kirsty then slipped her hand under her pillow

and brought forth the mouth-organ that Andy had left with her. Putting the instrument to her lips she produced a gay medley of tunes and Jean, not to be outdone, wrapped a piece of toilet tissue round her comb and joined with Kirsty in her impromptu little concert.

"My comb! Get me my comb, Nurse!" cried Meg excitedly. "I can't remember when I last played in a comb orchestra."

The nurse in question happened to be the formidable Isabel McLeod who had come back on duty, and with a grim smile she said meaningfully, "The simple little word 'please' was always used in *our* house, Mrs Munroe, and it would stand you in good stead if you learned to use it now and then."

"Ach, you're a hard, hard lassie," said Meg grumpily. "All right, please, please, may I have my comb and a piece of tissue – and don't take too long about it . . . if you would be so good, that is."

A smile broke the severity of Nurse McLeod's craggy features so that suddenly she looked young and not at all like the strict ogre she had seemed in the beginning.

"You're an old devil," she said with a shake of her head but went to get Meg's comb from her locker. The old lady seized it and blew into it with gusto and very soon the ward echoed with Scottish airs and melodies.

Some of the younger patients listened with

glowing faces and two of the nurses, coming along with the tea trolley, paused halfway up the ward to perform a little dance. Altogether, the atmosphere in the ward had considerably lightened and brightened.

"Nothing like a wee sing-song to pep up the blood," Meg said with a grin when she eventually had to pause for breath.

"A refreshment might pep it up even further." Nurse McLeod, cap askew and slightly out of breath from her exertions on the "dance floor" had stopped at Meg's bed with the tea trolley.

"*Gavee me drama*," Meg said in perfectly understandable Gaelic and Nurse McLeod, delighted to hear her native tongue, poured a measure of whisky from a bottle on the trolley and delivered it into Meg's willing hands. "This is better than tea any day," she said, and holding up her glass she cried, "*Slancha va*," which is the Gaelic for "good health".

Jean, hearing these exchanges, broke into a string of Gaelic expressions and soon she and Meg and Nurse McLeod were chattering away like long-lost cousins till the latter suddenly realised that the tea was getting cold and went rushing away up the ward somewhat red in the face.

"Where did you learn to speak Gaelic, Meg?" asked Jean as she sipped her orange juice.

"I used to work in the canteen of a western

isles ferry and as most of the crew were from the Hebrides I soon picked it up."

This was all too much for Miss Alice Kennedy. First that dreadful noise they all seemed to accept as music, then that old devil drinking whisky as if it were water and now . . . now, she and that surly Nurse McLeod gabbling away together in the Gaelic like old friends! It oughtn't to be allowed! Serving strong drink in a hospital ward! She herself had been shocked the first time she had been offered a glass of whisky and had made haste to let her disapproval be known. But it soon transpired that whisky or Guinness stout was indeed on the hospital "menu", so to speak, and anyone wishing to imbibe was at perfect liberty to do so.

"It's a disgrace, a disgrace!" she had complained to her long-suffering sister at visiting hour.

"The people here are dreadfully ill, Alice," Prudence Menzies had said reasonably. "And taken in moderation, whisky or stout can be a very good pick-me-up." Prudence knew only too well the truth of her words. When he had been alive her husband and herself had enjoyed a little Saturday-night refreshment in the privacy of their own home and no harm had ever come of it.

"And I seem to remember," she had gone on with a slight flush on her pleasant, honest face, "you yourself enjoying a brandy whenever you felt the need for it."

"Medicinal! Entirely medicinal!" Alice had exploded indignantly. "Completely refined and dignified and only to steady my heart. You know that perfectly well, Prudence, and should be ashamed of yourself for such unworthy observations."

Knowing it was useless to argue further, Prudence had held her counsel, leaving her sister with the satisfaction of having had, as usual, the last word.

And now this, Miss Alice Kennedy muttered to herself. That dreadful newcomer, Meg Munroe! Downing whisky in a most disgusting manner and winning friends as if she had been here for years. It wasn't right. It wasn't proper. It was just too much for a decent body to bear. She dealt with the situation in the manner she knew best. With a loud and huffy "Hmph!" she turned her back on her opponent and glared belligerently into space.

Jean and Kirsty choked back their snorts of amusement. Old Meg, though her eyes were twinkling, put a finger to her lips and warned them to hush. She was wise in the ways of the world. She felt sorry for Miss Alice Kennedy for she knew that her attitude to life had been caused by years of loneliness and Meg, despite the fact that her tongue often ran away with her, was possessed of a soft heart that was quick to melt and slow to harden.

Jean looked at Kirsty. "I hope I'm like Meg

when I grow old," she said thoughtfully. "She's such an interesting character and good fun into the bargain."

Jean's eyes went to the window. Her favourite sort of clouds were scudding across the sky, white and fluffy and edged with purple. When I grow old, she thought, I'll try not to grumble and always look upon the bright side.

"But if no bright side you can see, then polish up the dark side." Kirsty had only murmured the words but it was as if she had read Jean's thoughts.

Both girls stared at one another.

"One day we'll see rainbows together," Jean whispered. "Big and bold and beautiful and arched across the sky in bright shimmering colours."

Kirsty nodded. She couldn't wait to see Jean's rainbows for herself and hoped freedom would come soon for both of them.

Chapter 8

Miss Alice Kennedy knew that she didn't have very long to live. A crotchety lady at the best of times, she had become even more so with illness. She might be old but life was still sweet to her and as the days passed, bringing her closer to death, she had become more and more irritable.

But that was before Meg had appeared on the scene. Miss Kennedy had found out that her rival was also terminally ill and Miss Kennedy had begun to feel a grudging admiration for Meg's persistent cheerfulness in the face of personal trauma.

She began to wonder how she could break the icy barriers that she had erected between Meg and herself. She couldn't just change overnight. She had her pride to consider; it would never do to let the other woman think for one moment that she had won "the battle".

If you can't beat them, join them, she eventually decided and shortly afterwards she accepted "a very small whisky" from the drinks trolley, "for medicinal purposes only, of course," she intoned primly to no one in particular.

This was much to the amusement of Kirsty and Jean who had never imagined old Alice giving in to "vice", a favourite expression of hers and one that applied to many things that didn't quite meet with her approval.

As time went on an uneasy truce formed between Meg and Alice. Although they were by no means kindred spirits Miss Kennedy had begun to smile sourly at Meg's whimsical speech and outspoken comments. Meg on the other hand did *not* display any sort of pleasure when Miss Kennedy was in one of her "mightier than thou" moods. Instead she ignored her, leaving the other to "stew in her own juice".

Cantankerous Miss Kennedy didn't like this one bit. Nevertheless she believed that "someone of her standing" should never have to go cap in hand to "a little squirt like Meg Munroe and there was an end to the matter".

Meg, however, wouldn't kowtow to an old snob like Alice Kennedy. Only when she thought that "the upstart" had been given enough of the cold shoulder did she unbend and graciously allow herself to be won over.

The friendship developed further as both old ladies confided more and more in one another and even began to share reminiscences about their very different backgrounds. They drank their "wee drams" together and one evening, much to everyone's astonishment, Miss Kennedy suggested they play a game of cards.

She was a wizard in that particular field, shuffling the cards and dealing them with lightning speed. Very soon Miss Alice Kennedy had an ardent following. Each night, the patients who were allowed out of bed, including Kirsty and Jean, gathered round to watch the two ladies battling it out at cards. Meg was just as sharp as her opponent. To hear her witty comments and to watch Alice's cunning playing, was entertaining to say the least.

The minister's daughter blossomed amidst all the attention. She opened up, she smiled, she talked, she regaled one and all with romantic tales of her girlhood, reeling off so many names of old flames that even the younger women of the ward looked shocked.

"But you used to make out you were such a prude!" exclaimed one. "You turned up your nose when my boyfriend held my hand at visiting."

"Stuff and nonsense!" Alice said with spirit. "I was jealous, that was all. No one comes to hold *my* hand at visiting."

"Didn't your father object to all those boys in your life?" asked Meg who was rather stunned by her friend's true confessions.

Alice emitted one of her horse-like snorts. "Hmph! He was too busy and too wrapped up in himself to notice. Anyway, I was careful. Not even my sister Prudence knows the half of it so keep it under your hat."

"Why did you never marry?" Jean asked in her soft voice.

The old lady's eyes grew thoughtful. "I was engaged to be married, he was killed in the war. He was the only one of the bunch worth his salt. Never considered anyone else after him. Maybe that was unwise. Loneliness is like acid, it corrodes the spirit and eats away at the heart. In the end there's nothing worthwhile left."

Meg gripped her mottled hand. "Ay, there is," she said with a grin, "there's Jean and Kirsty – and there's me. We've a score to settle, Alice my lass, so stop feeling sorry for yourself and deal the cards. Give me a chance to beat *you* for a change."

Kirsty and Jean grew to love Alice and Meg and did all that they could for them. Both girls were now up and about: Jean's wound had healed well, her treatment had been reduced, the colour had returned to her cheeks.

"I'll get home soon," she told her parents and her brothers when they came to visit. "So don't you go using my bike, Jim Anderson, you broke it the last time and I was the one who was left to fix it."

Jim just smiled his easy-going smile, Mr and Mrs Anderson looked delighted at their daughter's returning health. Rob winked at Kirsty and told her he hoped she didn't boss her brother about the way Jean did hers. Kirsty laughed at this – Andy wasn't the sort of boy to let anyone take advantage of him, not even a sister whose illness was a constant source of worry to him.

"You're getting better," he said with relief on one of his visits. "You've got that cheeky look about you again."

"At least I'm not an old grump like some people I could name," was her quick retort.

"No, you're too busy being an angel in disguise," he returned drily, to which she laughed outright, glad to be feeling as good as she did.

Dr Kominski had spoken to her only that morning, telling her that she was responding well to treatment and if all went as well as he was hoping she would be going home sooner than he had at first thought.

"My hair hasn't come out," she told Andy delightedly. "Dr Kominski said it doesn't always happen." She paused then went on, "Quick, before Mum comes in, how are things with her and Dad?"

"While he was on leave, it was like old times, both of them the best of pals. Now it's back to square one. Last weekend they were at it again, nag, nag, nag."

"If we moved to Aberdeen to be beside Dad it would solve everything."

"No it wouldn't," Andy said sharply. "Mum can't leave Gran, Gran won't go to more sheltered housing and *I* certainly don't want to just up and leave my school and my mates."

"I wouldn't mind," Kirsty said in a small voice.

"I told you, Kirsty, you see it all through rose-coloured glasses. It's all right for you, you'll be leaving *your* school soon anyway. It wouldn't work for the rest of us. You're just a kid, everything's plain and simple to you."

"No it isn't!" she said hotly. "And I'm not a kid, I'm bigger than you sometimes, all you can think about is yourself."

"That's not true, I'm thinking about Mum and Gran and all the rest of it."

"I'll ask Gran what she would like next time she comes."

"Do that, you'll get the same answers as Mum did."

He glared at Kirsty. She was white and upset-looking and immediately he was ashamed of himself. "Look, sis," he said awkwardly, "I'm sorry, I didn't mean to shout at you, just you get better and come home, it will all sort itself out in the end."

But when Kirsty spoke to her gran she wasn't so sure about that.

"Would you like to move to Aberdeen, Gran?" she asked.

Granny Reid's lips folded into a grim line. "Not to more sheltered housing, I'm fed up with old people. Now, if it was to Red Rowans that would be different."

"Red Rowans." Kirsty murmured the name with affection.

"Ay, Red Rowans, I was so happy there as a girl. However . . ." she shrugged her shoulders disgustedly, "your mother won't hear o' it, says it's too big and would be too much work for her – as if we were all handless and couldn't help out. So – that's that as far as I'm concerned."

"Ay, that's that," Kirsty whispered dejectedly and said no more on the subject.

When old Alice died the ward was terribly upset. Only Meg seemed unmoved by the event. "Ach, she had it coming," was her verdict, delivered in a gravelly hard voice. "Her time was up, it happens to us all."

Later that day Kirsty noticed that the old lady was very quiet, her back was turned, her hanky was up at her eyes and she was crying.

Jean and Kirsty went to sit by the bed. "Please don't, Meg," Jean said with tears in her own eyes. "If it hadn't been for you she would have died without ever getting to know any of us."

"That's right," supplemented Kirsty, "and we wouldn't have discovered the *real* Miss Kennedy. You brought out a side of her that was funny and human. When she went to sleep last night she was happy, thanks to you."

Meg wiped her eyes and blew her nose with a flourish. "Ach, you're right. It's just – well, to tell the truth I'll miss the old dragon. She kept me on my toes and made me feel alive. Never mind . . ." she smiled and a sparkle had returned to her eyes. "I still have my lassies to keep me company. Go and fetch your teacups and I'll read the leaves for you. My mother read mine when I was a girl and to this day I remember how exciting it was to listen to the magic she spun for me."

The girls were entranced by Meg's predictions for their future. With her specs on the end of her nose she examined each cup in turn and with many ah-ha's and oh-ho's she purported to see journey's to exotic lands, glittering careers, and, lurking in the distance, two tall handsome strangers, one destined to become a husband to a young lady whose name began with the initial J, the other to a girl with the initial . . . "Now, is that a 'B' or an 'R'?" Meg, her brow wrinkled in concentration, prolonged the suspense.

Kirsty played the game, she wrung her hands and held her breath, letting it go in a drawn-out hiss when Meg finally announced with a triumphant shout, "It's a 'K'. Ay, he's definitely your man, Kirsty, though you'll have to wait a while before you can get your hands on him."

Kirsty laughed. "*He's* the one who'll have to wait. Before I even think about getting married I'm going to travel to all those foreign lands you spoke about . . ."

The rest of her words remained suspended. A girl was coming up the ward, none other than Mary Blair of "Dr Ogre" fame.

Mary was dragging her feet, she looked ill at

ease and her eyes were darting about the ward, as if she expected some dark and terrible creature to pounce on her at any moment.

"Oh, no," Kirsty said with a groan, "Mary Blair, she's two classes below me in school. All she ever does is giggle and say silly things. At least, that's how she used to be, now she looks scared to death half the time and tells gory doctor stories."

Kirsty went to sit by her bed to receive her visitor while Jean, who had heard all about Mary and wanted to hear more from "the horse's mouth", as it were, went back to bed where she pretended to read a book whilst keeping her ears well cocked.

Mary had brought a tray of fruit and a large "get well" card signed by Kirsty's classmates.

"It's a bit belated," Mary said in a breathless voice. "I – well – to tell the truth I should have brought it last week but I just never seemed to find the time. It's quite a long way to the hospital and Mum wouldn't let me come by myself so my Uncle Billy came with me. He's waiting downstairs." Her manner was nervous as she stood beside Kirsty, declining to sit down, refusing the grapes that Kirsty offered from a bowl of fruit at her bedside.

"No, I won't stay long if you don't mind. I promised Mum I'd be home by four-thirty."

"But, it's nearly that now – and you've only just got here."

"I know — that's what I mean," Mary replied in some confusion.

Just at that moment Dr Kominski passed down the ward in a brisk and businesslike manner.

Mary stared after him with round eyes. "He looks a bit fierce," she observed in a theatrical whisper. "He looks like . . ."

"Count Dracula," supplied Jean who had been longing to break into the conversation.

Mary reddened. "N-no, not exactly. I was going to say he looks a bit like the doctor who attended me for my appendix."

"Oh, you mean Doc Ogre," Kirsty said with a knowing nod. "Well, you're nearly right. It's his brother — identical twins, you see."

"Really?" Mary looked as if she was about to faint. Her face had gone pale, she took frequent glances over her shoulder, and was so altogether jumpy that Kirsty half expected her to get down on her knees at any moment to look under the beds.

"Listen, I hate hospitals," Mary confessed. "I only agreed to come with the fruit and stuff because everyone else thought I would know the ropes." She looked intently at Kirsty, "Promise you won't tell if I tell you a secret."

"I promise," Kirsty said solemnly.

"Truth is I've never been in hospital," Mary blabbered in a rush, "I only said that to make myself feel important. I wanted people to notice me instead of telling me to shut up every time I giggled. I only did that to get attention because at home my younger brothers and sisters get it all. I *did* have what my own doctor called a grumbling appendix. That was why I was absent from school." She sniffed. "There was no Doc Ogre – just me and my silly stories – I made it all up."

There was silence for a moment as Kirsty and Jean looked at one another, then they told Mary to sit down, relax and eat some fruit.

"It was a brilliant story," said Jean, her green eyes flashing. "It takes a bit of imagination to make up things like that."

"Jean's right," agreed Kirsty. "Who knows, maybe one day you'll become a famous writer."

"You think so? You really think so?" gabbled Mary, popping grapes into her mouth at such speed she choked and proceeded to cough and splutter for fully five minutes.

Meg opened one eye. "Ach, send for Dr Ogre," she said with a perfectly straight face. "Anybody can see the lass is dying and he is always good at a death."

Mary stopped coughing, Kirsty and Jean looked at Meg then at each other and finally at the red-faced Mary. They snorted, Meg gave a witch-like cackle, Mary released a high-pitched giggle. One and all gave vent to yells of merriment the like of which hadn't been heard in the ward for many a day. Mary hadn't enjoyed herself so much for a long time and she was loath to leave but the tea trolley had arrived.

Jean watched her walking away down the ward, "She's lonely is Mary, she needs someone to listen to her. I hope she comes back to see us."

"So do I." Kirsty sounded thoughtful. She had seen Mary in a different light that day; someone who craved friendship and made up silly stories in an effort to be noticed.

There and then Kirsty vowed that she would try and spend more time with Mary when she got out of hospital. She picked up the remains of her bunch of grapes. Mary had stripped it clean and it looked like a little bush shorn of its leaves. "So do I," she repeated and smiled reflectively at the memory of Mary and her Dr Ogre.

Chapter 9

The cleaning lady was working her way up the ward with her mop and bucket. She had an elongated drip at the end of her nose and Kirsty and Jean had made bets as to which bed she would reach before the drip parted company with its owner.

The girls watched fascinated.

"Going! Going . . .!" Jean mouthed comically.

The cleaning lady arrived at the second last bed in the ward. She gave a little cough and her drip landed straight into her bucket.

"Gone!" Jean said.

"Great shot!" Kirsty added.

They both erupted into stifled giggles, Jean drumming her heels against her mattress in her merriment. The cage around her legs had been removed some time ago and she was in great fettle.

Kirsty too was feeling more like her old self. Three weeks had gone by since her admittance to hospital. It had seemed like an eternity. The treatment she had been receiving had often made her feel sick and lethargic though she knew she would have felt much worse if it hadn't been for Jean. Meg too had been a source of great comfort. Even though she was very frail she still remained cheerful. She was always thinking of the girls and had boosted up their spirits when they had been flagging.

Dr Kominski came marching up the ward, almost tripping over the cleaning lady's bucket on the way. She threw him a sour look and took out her hanky to mop her nose before half-heartedly resuming her work.

The doctor made straight for the girls' beds and rubbing his hands briskly together he said jubilantly, "Good news! Your operation and subsequent treatment was well worthwhile, Jean. Your X-rays show no signs of further tumours so we'll keep our fingers crossed that the cancer cells have been wiped out.

"As for you, Kirsty, your white blood count has edged towards normal which means that you are moving towards what we call remission; in other words, the drug treatment has given your leukaemia a good battering."

"Does that mean we can go home, Doctor?" asked Jean excitedly.

"We'll do a few more tests on the pair of you. If the results are satisfactory then I don't see any reason why both of you can't go home." The doctor smiled at their looks of jubilation. "We'll have you back periodically just to keep tabs on you and make sure everything is OK. All you have to do is take things easy for a while although that doesn't mean you can't go on with your lives as normal."

A great surge of energy pounded through Kirsty's body. She felt as if she wanted to leap out of bed and proclaim her delight to the world. Instead she lay back on the pillows and treated Dr Kominski to a radiant smile. The sunshine had come back into her life again and everything was wonderful in those moments. She wanted to share it with everyone but most of all with her parents and Andy and Granny Reid, all of whom had been such faithful visitors during her hospital stay.

The only thing was . . . her parents had as yet to make a firm decision about the future – whether to stay in Paisley or move to Aberdeen. They were all still arguing about it and sometime, somehow, they would all have to make up their minds.

She didn't stay gloomy for long however. The very next morning both she and Jean received the news that they were to go home. Kirsty made a dive for the phone to tell her mother to bring her clothes while Jean lost no time packing the suitcase that she had brought with her to hospital. Her parents had a long journey to make from Sanda. They had to rely on a ferry to the mainland and then a train to Glasgow so it had been arranged that Jean would spend a night with Kirsty before travelling back home with her family.

"Oh, I can hardly wait to see it all again!" Jean tossed a strand of fair hair away from a face that was pink with excitement. She grabbed Kirsty's arm. "You and Andy *must* come for a holiday, Kirsty. We could have a great time. Sanda is a mix of sun, wind and showers, and fantastic rainbows. Sometimes, when you look out over the Atlantic Ocean, you can see two rainbows merging into one another and through them are little islands, purple and blue and green, fairytale lands that don't seem to belong to the world."

Kirsty's imagination was fired by Jean's wonderful descriptions of her home. "You make it all sound so exciting, Jean, so clear and real. I feel as if I'm there on Sanda when you talk about it."

"I listen to the old folks," Jean explained. "I've always been interested in the history of the islands. It's great fun to visit the old people and hear the stories that have been passed down through the generations."

So absorbed were the girls with one another they had forgotten Meg. She was lying back on her pillows, a little sad-looking as she listened to their youthful chatter and their future plans.

"I'm glad you two are such good friends," she said kindly. "I had a pal all my life and I always knew I could trust her and tell her anything. She died last year and I miss her so much."

"We're your friends, Meg," Jean said quickly.

"And we'll never forget you," Kirsty added. "You know that, don't you?"

"Ay, of course I do, the pair of you have kept me going these last few weeks. I don't know what I'd have done without you."

The girls glanced at one another. They knew they would never see Meg again. She was very ill and was small and fragile-looking in the cocoon of her pink fluffy bedjacket.

But a smile was never far from her mouth. Seeing their sad expressions she held out her thin little hands to them and they clasped one each as she went on in a whisper, "You've made an old woman happy. I know I haven't got long to go but you're both young with all your lives in front of you. Give it all you've got and enjoy yourselves to the full." Her eyes closed. "As you go back to your different worlds, remember these words: 'Be good, sweet maids, and let who will be wicked.'"

"It's difficult always to be good, Meg," said Kirsty, not quite understanding what the old lady meant.

Jean made a face. "I can't help being wicked sometimes. My brothers often call me a witch and used to pretend to burn me at the stake when we were little."

An appreciative smile flitted over Meg's face. "Ay, you're right, it's very dull being good *all* the time. I never was, but at my age I'm expected to be full of goodness and light and to say all the right things to young people."

Her eyes popped open and suddenly they were bird-bright and alive with devilment. "Did I set a good example to you two? Have I been a paragon of virtue? Was I every inch a pink and white old lady of impeccable behaviour and sweet nature?"

"You were very good at cards," Kirsty said with a giggle.

Meg's fingers tightened in their hands, then they grew loose as her eyes closed once more.

The girls held on to her till she slept. Their joined hands made a little triangle of love that reached down to comfort her even in her dreams.

It was Saturday morning and the sounds of guitar and flute filled the air. Kirsty was singing "A Bunch of Thyme" and Andy was playing the harmony part. Mrs McKinnon was cleaning the living-room windows while she enjoyed the music and hummed little snatches of it under her breath.

Kirsty had been home two weeks now. She looked well and was full of bounce and her mother found it hard to believe that anything had ever been wrong with her.

It had been a worrying time for them all, made worse by the fact that Mr McKinnon seemed to be away more than ever these days. He hadn't come home this weekend, making the excuse that they were short-staffed and that he had been asked to stay behind to help out.

"Can't you try *not* to fight all the time?" Andy said to his mother. "If you won't go to stay in Aberdeen and he can't find work here you have to come to a compromise."

"It's not as easy as that, Andy," his mother retaliated. "Things have got out of hand somehow. What with Gran refusing to move with us if we go to another house that isn't Red Rowans, you being so stubborn about staying here . . ."

"Just like you, Mum," Andy said quickly.

"Yes, Andy, just like me. Kirsty is the only one among us who seems not to mind one way or another."

Kirsty did mind, she knew what she wanted, but she didn't want to complicate matters even further by saying so, and so she said nothing.

The postman was coming up the street and Mrs McKinnon went to the hall to gather up the little pile of mail from the hair rug, thumbing through it quickly to see if there was a letter from her husband. Sometimes he wrote to her if he couldn't manage to get home but this time there was nothing, though his familiar hand *was* there on an envelope addressed to Kirsty and Andy.

"Letter from Dad!" Mrs McKinnon called. "And another for you, Kirsty, all to yourself."

Brother and sister devoured the letter from

their father before Kirsty turned her attention to the other. Tearing it open she read the first few lines and shouted, "It's from Jean! She wants Andy and me to come to Sanda when the school holidays start! Can we go, Mum?'

"Of course you can go, it will do you the world of good to get away. All that sea air on Sanda is just the thing you need."

"What about you?" Andy said slowly. "You need a break as well."

"I couldn't get the time off work and someone has to look after the house and the cat . . . Besides, your father might easily get some holidays and someone has to be here. We still love one another you know, Andy . . ." She hesitated then went on, "Perhaps I've been unreasonable, if Gran agreed – and you too, Andy – we might be happier all round if we moved. Not to Red Rowans though, it's a barn of a place and we'd freeze in the winter."

"Gran won't agree," Kirsty spoke suddenly. "I spoke to her in the hospital, and she's set her heart on Red Rowans."

Mrs McKinnon sighed. Andy turned to his sister and gave her a little push. "Come on, it's time to go. We're late enough as it is. It's a twelve-o-clock kick-off and you'd better be there in goal or there'll be trouble." Grabbing their bags and boots they rushed away, leaving Mrs McKinnon to pick up the letter they had received from their father. On the last page, at the end, he had said he would write to her soon.

Well, she wasn't going to wait for that. Her talk with Andy had helped her make up her mind, that and the look of strain on Kirsty's face. Andy was right, a decision had to be reached, and the sooner the better for all of them.

She picked up the phone and dialled her husband's number. His voice came over the line. "It's me, Bob," she said with a catch in her throat. "I've made up my mind. We'll sell up here and move to Aberdeen. I can't stand being without you any longer."

He laughed. "You always were full of surprises. I'm delighted, Jan, I'm always thinking about you and miss you and the children. How did you manage to persuade your mother?"

"I haven't – I – my place is with you – I should have realised that sooner."

There was a long silence. "You can't do it, Jan. You can't leave your mother behind. You would feel guilty all the time and start worrying about her."

"I'll talk to her."

"You know what her answer will be. She won't come and live with us in a house that isn't Red Rowans."

"I can't do it, Bob. I liked that house for the holidays but that's all. If we went there I'd never have a spare moment to myself. We would need

93

a housekeeper to make it work and we certainly couldn't afford that."

"If we sold our own house we would have enough money for all the alterations needed. Your mother could have her own flat inside the house. We would make it so that everything is modernised and easy for you to run."

"Let me think about it, Bob."

"All right, but not for too long. I want to come home every night to you and the kids."

"See you soon?"

"Next weekend."

"Andy and Kirsty have been invited to Sanda for a holiday in a few weeks' time."

"Great, just what Kirsty needs."

"I'll count the days till I see you, Bob." She put down the phone and stood gazing round the room, so comfortable and clean, so cosy. She thought of Red Rowans; draughty, cold and dark, and she shivered.

PART TWO

Sanda

Chapter 10

Muckle McPhee helped to secure the ropes as the ferry swayed and bumped against the pier. There were a fair number of passengers at this time of the year and Muckle liked nothing better than to be there to nod a welcome to everybody as they came down the gangway, laden with cases and other holiday gear.

The harbour was a favourite place for many of the old men of the island. Always there was a buzz of activity of some kind: fishermen mending their nets; boats of all sorts plying in and out; stoutly-booted young men unloading their lobster pots; supplies coming off the ferry.

And of course there was the wonderfully exhilarating smells of the harbour: tar and brine, the tang of the sea mingling with that of peat smoke drifting from the chimneys; the pungent odours of slimy wood and fish scales; the scent of wild broom blowing down from the hills.

Over and above all were the sounds of the sea: the gulls crying from above; curlews calling from the shore; the plaintive voices of lapwings from the fields . . . and the skylarks, ecstatically trilling on high, never-ending notes of delight for summer and sun, sea and sky.

Some of the more ancient islanders were content just to sit on the harbour walls, smoking their pipes and making desultory conversation as they watched the world go by.

Not so Muckle. He enjoyed activity and liked to be in the centre of things. He was a giant of a man, broad-shouldered and tightly muscled; his beard was long and flowing, his eyebrows bushy and wild, the deep blue of his eyes a startling feature in his nut-brown face.

He had spent most of his young manhood at sea and had remained a bachelor saying that he had never found the right girl to marry, though it wasn't for want of trying on the part of the ladies. "A woman would just ruin me with her wants and her wiles," he would laugh whenever anyone asked him why he had never married. "And I'm too long in the tooth to want to change my ways now."

Jean's dad had told her that Muckle was the strongest man he had ever met. A favourite story at island ceilidhs concerned his rescue of a young girl whose foot had been trapped in a large anchor buried in the sandy shallows of the bay. The tide had been rising and she would have drowned had not Muckle appeared on the scene to grab the anchor and wrench it clear. In a feat of amazing strength he had lifted it as if it were a feather and had thrown it almost three metres away where it remained to the present day, a crumbling testimonial to his manly might. Others had tried to raise the anchor but it had resisted all attempts to move it. "Muckle's Anchor", as it came to be called, was now part of local history. Small boys pointed it out proudly to visiting relatives, old worthies included it in their repertoire of fireside tales, tourists wandered to the bay to gape at it and to take snapshots for the holiday album.

Muckle was one of Jean's favourite people and she went to take his arm as she waited for her friends to come off the boat.

Kirsty came first, her face glowing as she rushed down to give Jean a welcoming embrace. The girls gazed at one another, delighted to meet again, while Muckle went forward to help Andy who was grumbling a bit as he struggled to carry the cases and the musical instruments they had brought with them.

"Are you going to give us a tune?" Muckle asked in his warm, friendly voice.

"I don't think I've got any wind left," Andy said breathlessly. "Kirsty was *supposed* to help with the luggage."

"Oh, don't be such a moaner." Kirsty spoke with a laugh as she came over to her brother. "It's so good to be here."

Her sparkling eyes surveyed it all, the hills, the sky, the deep blue of the ocean, all just as Jean had described it. She threw out her arms as if to embrace Sanda to her bosom and Andy, catching her mood, gazed around him appreciatively. Taking out his flute he began to play "The Mingulay Boat Song", much to the delight of the crowd milling about on the pier. Kirsty took her guitar from its case and joined in with her brother, everyone clapped and the captain of the ferry gave a loud toot on the ship's horn.

Muckle grinned and took a flask from his pocket. "Here's to Kirsty and Andy," he cried. '*Slainte* and welcome to Sanda. I can see we're in for a good time with you two around and I'll come over to Croft an Cala whenever I can, to join in your fun."

It had been raining, everything looked clean and newly washed, the sea was sparkling, distant islands merged into the mist on the horizon.

Kirsty stood at the window and took a deep breath. Her first morning on Sanda, a wonderful, pearly-blue morning filled with light and space and rays of sunshine filtering down from the sky to splash gold on the waves ... The birds were singing, a spider's web outside the window glistened with diamond-like dewdrops, a tiny wren was searching for insects in the roof gutters ...

And then she saw her first rainbow, shimmering and bright, arched across the great dome of the sky.

She held her breath and as she watched another rainbow appeared, a reflection of the first, fainter than the other but still hazily bright and beautiful.

Kirsty put her hand to her mouth. "An island of rainbows," she whispered.

The smell of bacon and eggs came wafting up from the kitchen. Kirsty suddenly felt ravenously hungry and she lost no time getting downstairs. Robbie, Jim, and Andy were already seated at the table, chattering away like long-lost pals.

A large orange and white cat came to wrap itself round Kirsty's legs while a black and white collie dog, not to be outdone, bounded over to take her fingers in his mouth and pull her into the room.

Mrs Anderson turned a hot face from the stove. "Good morning, Kirsty, you mustn't mind Sam. He thinks he's the boss around here since he retired from the fields. Come away in and sit yourself down. Jean's out feeding the hens but she'll be back in a moment."

Mr Anderson's big frame darkened the doorway. Stooping, he removed his mud-caked boots and hung his cap on a hook beside a motley collection of ancient jackets. He then went to the sink to give his hands a quick wash.

"We *do* have soap, Alan,' Mrs Anderson laughed.

He had green eyes the same as his daughter and at that moment they were twinkling. "Waste not, want not," he replied with a chuckle. "I'll only get them dirty again later so might as well save the soap till bedtime."

Jean came rushing in to hurl cold water over her hands before drying them hurriedly on the kitchen towel.

Mrs Anderson had to smile. "Like father, like daughter, you two are a fine example to set to visitors."

Jean looked at her father, he gazed back at her and they both grinned at one another and helped themselves to toast.

Kirsty glanced round at all the faces. She liked the Anderson family, they were friendly and funny and very, very natural . . .

"Bless this food and make us good,
Help us to laugh, love and live,
and feel compassion to forgive."

Mrs Anderson had sat down and she was saying grace. The hands of Jean and her father were suspended suddenly above the toast rack. Jean's face was red with suppressed mirth, that of Mr Anderson was no better.

Jean caught Kirsty's eye and Kirsty had to lower her head quickly. She mustn't snort, she simply could *not* snort because then Jean would follow suit and that would be a fine start to her very first morning at Croft an Cala, which was Gaelic for Croft of the Haven.

Outside the larks were singing, the cows were

grazing, the hens were crooning peacefully below the window.

It *was* a haven, a delightful place to be this bright and sunny morning. Mrs Anderson had a very nice voice, soft and sort of blurred at the edges.

"Amen," she said and removed the cover from the dish of bacon.

"Amen," everyone echoed.

"Lovely bacon," Robbie said in the same breath.

Kirsty giggled. She knew she was going to enjoy her holiday at Croft an Cala.

Kirsty was looking thoughtful as she helped Jean wash up the breakfast dishes. "I like your parents, Jean, they're so friendly."

"I know. I'm lucky with Mum and Dad but they do have their arguments and sometimes Dad loses his temper altogether and goes stomping out of the house."

Kirsty nodded. "I used to think mine were perfect till Dad got a job in Aberdeen which changed everything. He and Mum began arguing because he wasn't home all the time.'

Jean leaned against the sink and looked at her friend. "Isn't it strange, Kirsty, you and me, meeting in hospital? Old Meg and Alice, starting off at loggerheads with each other then ending up old pals. I feel so well now I can hardly remember what it was like being ill."

"Me neither, though it all came flooding back when I had to go to the hospital for a check-up."

"I've been for one as well, all clear. Mum was so pleased she took me into town and bought me a blouse and some new shorts . . ."

She looked beyond the window to the sea sparkling in the distance . . . "It's a bonny day. The boys said something about going over to the islands. We'll get the donkeys saddled up and have a marvellous time."

Chapter 11

Monty and Jeremy were two big fluffy donkeys with smiling faces and happy dispositions. They had been with the Anderson family for three years and though they didn't mind being used for light farm work they much preferred fun and games and liked nothing better than to go adventuring with the children.

Today it was the beach which meant a good gambol in the cool sea water, and as soon as the saddles appeared Monty rolled back his lips to give vent to a loud "hee-haw" as the straps were being fixed round his considerable girth.

While Jean and Kirsty filled a picnic basket with home-made jammy scones and flasks of lemonade the boys went to the shed to get the bikes, large upright ancient affairs with squeaky wheels and rusty frames. But the tyres and brakes were in good working order though Robbie inflated all the tyres just to make certain they wouldn't let anyone down, so to speak.

Before they went off Jean filled a shallow basket with flowers from the garden which she arranged swiftly but tastefully in vases.

Mrs Anderson ruffled her hair. "You never forget, do you? But you're dashing about far too much. Remember what the doctor said."

Jean's radiant smile flashed out. "I feel wonderful, Mum, but I promise not to overdo it. I'll let Monty take the strain."

It had been decided to let the girls take the donkeys while the boys rode on the bikes and they set off, laughing and chattering, revelling in the fact that it was the holidays and that the sun was shining.

Their way took them down past the village with its whitewashed cottages and tiny walled gardens. At the post office they turned on to a single track road that led to the south of the island.

As they passed over a stone bridge at the foot of a steep hill they saw Hamish Grant sitting on a wall that skirted a daisy-strewn field. "Hallo!" he cried as the contingent drew nearer. "Are you going to the beach? Want some company?"

"The more the merrier," agreed Robbie.

"I'll just tell Gran where I'm going," said Hamish and went off to a tiny stone cottage with deeply recessed windows and a thatched roof.

Both his parents had been killed in a car crash when he was a baby and Hamish had come to live with his granny on Sanda. He was small for fourteen, wiry and strong and able to throw a stone further than any boy on the island – a fearsome contender at local highland games

106

where, competing with grown men, he invariably won the welly-boot-throwing contest.

He was soon back, grinning from ear to ear, his spiky red hair falling into his eyes. Without further ado Hamish climbed up beside Kirsty to share Jeremy's broad back.

"Jean was telling me all about you, Kirsty," he said conversationally. "How you met in hospital and became friends."

"That's right," Kirsty nodded. "If it hadn't been for her I don't know what I would have done. She kept me boosted up and put things into perspective for me."

"That's what she said about you. It must have been tough, discovering you had leukaemia, dealing with it the way you did."

There was a strong note of admiration in his voice and for the rest of the way they talked, telling one another about themselves.

They crossed the headland and it wasn't long before they were on Silversand Bay. Here the Atlantic waves spumed into great caverns in the cliffs and foamed around the reefs but the bay itself was calm and safe, the water a clear turquoise-blue in the sandy shallows. In the middle of the bay, sixty metres offshore, were the tidal isles known as the Freshnish Group, cut off only when the water was high, as it was now.

They dismounted and Jean slapped Monty on the rump. With a loud "hee-haw" he was off, galloping down the beach and straight into the sea. Hamish was in one of his wild moods. With a loud whoop he leapt once more on to Jeremy's back, followed closely by Jim, and the startled donkey took off. As it reached the water's edge it stopped suddenly and lowered its head, whereupon Hamish and Jim sailed straight over its neck and into the water. Jean and Kirsty were hysterical with laughter.

"Serves them right for showing off. Jim always was an idiot and Hamish is no better," commented Robbie though he couldn't help grinning as he added, "It's just like something from a Laurel and Hardy movie – and the donkeys certainly look as if they're enjoying the joke."

Jeremy and Monty were frolicking about in the shallows, braying loudly and baring their teeth in a delighted show of enjoyment.

The Anderson dinghy was retrieved from the little cave where it was kept. "I take it you know all about the tides and everything?" Andy said, addressing Robbie.

"Have no fear," Robbie said assertively. "We've been here all our lives, remember, and we know all there is to know about currents and tides. When the water is low you can walk straight over the sands to these islands. Just now the tide is high so we take the boat."

Soon they were all aboard and rowing out towards the Freshnish Isles. Passing the south tip of the biggest island they rowed straight into the Cave of the Echoes. It was like entering a cathedral: massive basalt pillars supported the entrance and the domed interior was so high that seabirds nested on the ledges and made a great racket as they swooped in and out.

"Hallo-ooo!" Kirsty cried and leapt back in fright as her voice echoed and rebounded from the rocky walls.

Andy took his flute from its case and began to play a medley of tunes. The notes were magnified in the wonderful acoustics of the cave and the echoes gave the impression that a dozen flutes were in full swing.

There was a plentiful supply of driftwood inside the cave and very soon Robbie and Andy between them had a fire going and had fixed up a length of string for a clothes line. Both Jim and Hamish were glad to strip off their sodden clothes and wrap themselves in beach towels, looking rather sheepish as they arranged their underpants and socks on the line after which they rushed to the fire to huddle over it.

"Never mind," laughed Jean. "Lunch should cheer you up. We've brought enough to feed an army."

In minutes, soup and potatoes were boiling in billycans set on top of flat stones at the edge of the fire. Jean served the meal in margarine tubs and when everything was eaten they all lay back replete.

But live-wire Hamish couldn't rest for long.

"I'm for a swim!" he yelled and without more ado he dived straight into the deep pool inside the cave. It was like a dark green lagoon. Fingers of sunlight cast reflections on the surrounding pink rock and the water was so clear it was possible to see shoals of tiny fish darting about below.

Hamish was soon joined by the others, Jean showed Kirsty how to float and before long they were all lying on their backs, rocking gently to and fro in water that was fed from the Gulf Stream and was therefore pleasantly warm.

In the course of the afternoon Hamish caught some large flounders by means of a little barbed harpoon-like attachment on his penknife. With this tied to the end of a long stick he was able to spear the fish as they came along.

His friends looked on in astonishment as he landed one catch after another until there were at least half a dozen fish lying at his feet on the rocks. "Dinner," he grinned in his cheeky fashion, "I'll clean and gut them and you lot can cook them while I rest from my labours."

Jim's deft hands had soon fashioned an old piece of fencing wire into a spit and in minutes the savoury aroma of sizzling fish was wafting through the cave.

Kirsty gazed all around her. The sunlight was shafting into the pool making dazzling reflections, the gulls were drifting about at the cave's entrance on wings of purest white, the faces surrounding the fire glowed golden in its light, and she thought how precious this wonderful day was after her long spell of illness in hospital.

Jean seemed to read her mind. Her hand came out to take Kirsty's and she squeezed it hard. Both girls just gazed at one another in silent acknowledgement of the freedom that was now theirs.

"Pioneers, that's how I think of us," said Jim as everyone gathered round the fire to eat the fish. "The food provided by Mother Nature — and Hamish too of course. You certainly know how to be self-sufficient. Maybe you'll teach me how to spear fish like that."

Everyone was sorry when it was time to go. Hamish was most attentive to Kirsty, steadying her as they climbed over the slippery rocks to the cave's entrance. Jean winked at Kirsty, making her blush a bright red which deepened even further as Hamish caught her hand and gallantly helped her in to the dinghy.

Everyone else clambered aboard and leaving the little sandy cove they paddled towards Silversand Bay. Kirsty looked back at the Fresh-nish Isles, her gaze lingering on the Cave of the Echoes. It had been a wonderful day, one that she knew she would always remember, no matter what else might happen to her in the future.

Jeremy and Monty were waiting patiently in the bay. Jean took one look at them and to the tune of "The Drunken Sailor" she began to sing.

> "We're so lucky to have two donkeys,
> We're so lucky to have two donkeys,
> We're so lucky to have two donkeys,
> To take us home in the evening."

They put the dinghy away and made their way home through the golden twilight, the donkeys walking with a steady rhythm, Kirsty dreamy and silent as she went over the day's happenings in her mind.

Jean made one or two attempts at conversation but soon fell silent, content just to be there with her friend. She felt at ease in Kirsty's company and respected her need for privacy but she couldn't help smiling when the time came for Hamish to say his farewells.

"I'll see you soon," he called at the gate. "I'll teach you how to spear fish, Jim – and you too, Kirsty."

The smile he flashed at her was warm and special. Jean waited till he was out of earshot before saying to her friend, "He's got it bad, Kirsty, and him only just turned fourteen."

Kirsty's face flared crimson once more. "Och, you," she scolded, turning away. Then she giggled. "He might not like me quite so much when he finds out I can spear fish with the best of them. Dad taught Andy and me when we used to spend holidays with Great-aunt Bella in the north of Scotland."

Jean stared. "Oh, but you'll hurt Hamish's feelings if he can't show off a bit to you. You know what boys are like."

"I know fine well," returned Kirsty, her dimples showing in her laughing face. "I've been playing their games and doing their kind of thing ever since I can remember, so don't worry on that score. I'll let Hamish show me how to spear fish – and I'll warn Andy not to say anything. Only thing is . . ." here she giggled again, "I can't promise not to get *better* than Hamish. That can happen, you know, a pupil overtaking her teacher, especially if the teacher is a good one and the pupil exceptionally brilliant!"

Chapter 12

The days on Sanda passed all too quickly for Kirsty and Andy. Never a moment was wasted, never a minute spent in boredom. They roamed the hills and walked the moors, they swam and sailed and rode the donkeys.

Making good use of the bikes they explored the island, had barbecues on the beach, picnicked anywhere and everywhere. No one wanted the holidays ever to end. When the weather was bad Jean took them visiting various crofts and cottages all over the island, and wherever they went the islanders welcomed them and plied them with tea and scones.

They helped Mr Anderson in the fields and enjoyed going to the harbour with Muckle to listen to his old cronies telling their tales of the sea in their slow, lilting Hebridean voices.

They had been on Sanda a week when it was decided to hold a ceilidh in the Anderson croft. The Anderson family were renowned for these social gatherings and on the night in question it seemed as if half the island had turned up.

Old Mac was there with his fiddle, Muckle

had brought his pipes, Joe McKenzie came with his accordion. There was also an assortment of other instruments including mouth-organs and in no time at all a good going sing-song was under way.

Kirsty played her guitar with Andy accompanying her on his flute, Jean sang, following up with a lively performance on the spoons. Mr Anderson's efforts on his accordion had everybody tapping their feet, the younger ones getting up to dance, "Hooching" and "Yooching" as they whirled around the room to the stirring melodies.

Mrs Anderson and Old Mac played their fiddles together, entrancing the gathering with wild Gypsy airs and plaintive sea shanties. Rob and Jim were persuaded to play the pipes and again the dancing was in full swing as it was quite impossible to resist the blood-stirring reels and strathspeys that the boys were producing.

By this time everybody was hot and breathless, windows and doors were thrown wide to allow the summer breezes into the house.

Mrs Anderson had provided a tempting array of food. For days, with the help of Kirsty and Jean, she had rolled dough and stirred batter till her arms were aching. The result was a table groaning with scones, cakes, pancakes, sausage rolls, oatcakes, crusty bread, salads and an assortment of cooked meats, and, in place of honour, an enormous whole salmon, pink and firm and tender.

Supper over, it was the time for the *seanachaidhs* to gather round the hearth. *Seanachaidh* is the Gaelic word for storyteller, usually a person of great age and wisdom with a lifetime of knowledge to their credit.

Robbie was the exception to the rule. From an early age he had soaked in the talk and the tales of his elders and though he was just fourteen he was held in great respect by the old men of the island and was always invited to join them at their gatherings.

Tonight he was politely asked to start off proceedings and reddened at the honour being bestowed upon him.

"Yes, go on, Rob," urged Jim who loved his brother's tales.

Kirsty and Jean pulled their chairs close to the hearth, cupped their chins in their hands and generally made themselves cosy and comfortable. A silence fell over the room while everyone waited for Robbie to begin. Gloaming had descended over the countryside. The sun had just sunk into the sea in a fiery ball, painting the sky in tones of brilliant orange and gold merging into wonderful hues of turquoise and lilac. The room was lit only by the fire's light and the afterglow of sunset and was a perfect atmosphere for mystical tales of the past.

Robbie had composed himself, his eyes very dark as he glanced round the room and said in his slow, lilting voice, "I am thinking of a time long, long ago when there was a village in the north of Scotland called Kalak Mar. Every year, in the month of May, there were great celebrations and some of the young girls would be chosen to become mermaids. It was considered a great honour to go and live with the seal people. At midnight the Seal Men would come ashore, doff their pelts, and dance with the villagers round the bonfires on the moonlit beach.

"Just before dawn, the Seal Men would vanish into the sea, taking with them their new mermaids. One young girl called Vera had been chosen to become a mermaid but she had fallen in love with a local fisherlad known as Iain Mara, which meant Iain of the Sea.

"Vera didn't want to leave him but her parents insisted that she go with the seal people as a refusal to do so would bring bad luck on the village. With tears streaming down her face she was carried away by the Seal Men but just before she disappeared under the waves she called back to her lover, 'Never forget me, Iain, we'll be reunited, some day we'll meet again.'

"Iain was devastated, the love of his life was gone, he knew he would never forget her. To the end of his days he would search the oceans and the seas and never give up hope of being with her again.

"Months went by and he was still pining and crying for his sweetheart. Life had lost all meaning for him and he no longer laughed and sang as he had done when he and Vera were together.

"Then one day a kelpie appeared beside him on the beach. Kelpies were fabulous creatures, able to turn themselves into real horses when ashore, and this one was no exception. Up the beach it galloped to where Iain was sitting, holding Vera's hair ribbon in his hand.

"Iain had been deep in thought and was startled by the appearance of the kelpie, especially when it raised its head and began to call in a seal-like voice.

" 'What are you trying to tell me?' asked Iain. 'Do you know where Vera is?'

"For answer the kelpie nodded its head and made a sign for Iain to jump on its back. This Iain did and like a streak of lightning the kelpie galloped down the beach and plunged straight into the sea to vanish beneath the waves.

"To this very day, on a moonlit night in the village of Kalak Mar, you can sometimes hear the laughter of a young boy and girl and if you go down to the beach you might see them, splashing about in the ocean, riding the waves, together again as Vera had wished on that fateful night of long ago when she was being carried away by the Seal Men to live under the waves."

The gathering was spellbound by the wonder of Robbie's words and when he came to the end of his tale no one spoke, as if afraid they might break the magic that his voice had cast over the room.

Kirsty was the first to find her tongue. "That was a wonderful story, Robbie, you made it sound so real. That bit about Vera being carried away by the seal people sent the shivers down my spine."

"Ay, you did right well, lad," Old Angus agreed, stroking his long beard thoughtfully. "But the story that I have in mind is very different from yours. It happened a long, long time ago, way back in the Dark Ages when witches and warlocks roamed these islands . . ."

And so it went on, the myths, the legends, the folklore. No one wanted the night to end and it was with great reluctance that they rose to go at midnight, piped out into the scented summer darkness by Muckle who was still in great fettle and would have gone on for hours yet if he had had his way.

Everyone had lent a hand helping Mrs Anderson to clear away the tables and wash the dishes so that all the family had to do was tumble into bed and fall asleep. But Kirsty and Jean were wide awake and the latter crept into Kirsty's room to snuggle down in bed beside her and relive the ceilidh all over again. "It was a wonderful evening," sighed Kirsty. "And Robbie's story was the best of all."

Jean gave vent to an enormous yawn. "I told

you that Sanda was a marvellous place. It's so lovely to have the holidays and you here, Kirsty. Sometimes I think of the hospital, the fear I had of losing my leg – and afterwards – waiting to see if all the cancer cells had gone. I used to wonder if I would ever get really better and when I was really down in the dumps I thought I might never see my island again."

Kirsty nodded in understanding. "I know, I was the same, afraid all the time, hardly able to believe what had happened to me, hating the drugs and the sickness and all the rest of it. The days were so long – and yet we made some good friends. I often think of old Meg and how she is."

"She was dying, Kirsty," said Jean sadly. "She knew she didn't have long to go, yet she was so thoughtful, helping us when we were low, bucking us up, keeping us amused with the funny things she said."

"A real character, as my gran would say. Do you ever look at old people and imagine what they were like long ago?'

"I know what you mean, their looks and everything," said Jean thoughtfully. "Meg had a nice face, kind and sort of youngish even though she was wrinkled. Going from what she said I suppose she led a full life when she was really young."

"It must be awful, to be old and ill – and – to die. I want to live till I'm at least a hundred, I have so much to see and do with my life. After being so ill I appreciate everything so much more."

"Me too, lots and lots of places to see, millions of things to do."

There was silence for a few moments, then Kirsty's voice came sleepily, "I wonder if we'll still be friends when we're both a hundred years old."

Jean snorted into the pillow. "Of course we will, silly, *and* we'll still go swimming and riding and play our guitars and fiddles. I might even be an old skinhead wearing a leather jacket and black leggings and have tattoos emblazoned on my bald head."

Kirsty let out a shout of laughter and for the next ten minutes they talked nonsense and almost smothered in the bedclothes in their attempts to muffle their sounds of merriment.

Then suddenly it was only the sigh of the sea and the cries of the night birds outside the window. Jean and Kirsty were asleep having talked and laughed themselves into exhaustion.

Chapter 13

The highlight of the holiday for both Kirsty and Andy came the next morning when Jean answered a knock at the door.

"*Dad!*" cried brother and sister in unison, "what are you doing here?"

Mr McKinnon's blue eyes twinkled. "That's an odd kind of welcome for a long lost father. Shall I go out and come back in again?"

"You dare!" said Kirsty, running to take his arm and pull him further into the room. "You're just such a big surprise, that's all. We didn't know you were coming or we would have been at the harbour to meet you."

"I didn't know I was coming myself until last night. Call it a spur of the moment decision if you like. It's so long since I've seen you both I felt I just had to make the journey to Sanda."

Placing his hands on Kirsty's shoulders he gazed at her for a long moment. "You look great, sweetheart, colour in your cheeks, your eyes bright. It's so good to see you back to your old self again."

"Dad, is everything all right?" Andy asked

impatiently, his initial happiness waning as he remembered the dissension that had existed between his parents.

Jean and Mrs Anderson had slipped discreetly from the kitchen, thus giving the McKinnons the freedom to talk openly.

"Everything is perfect," assured Mr McKinnon happily. "Your mother and I have been busy and I have a lot to tell you. But first things first, I'd love a cup of tea."

Kirsty saw that her father was elated about something and she had to know more. "Tell us now, Dad," she urged. "Is it about moving? Have you found a house near Aberdeen? Is it one that Gran will like?"

Mr McKinnon held up his hands. "Later, lass. I'm hot, tired and thirsty, and so far I haven't even been offered that cup of tea."

Kirsty rushed to put the kettle on. After that she and Andy set out to enjoy their father's visit to the full. He was only staying the one night and every moment was therefore precious. Jean was invited to come along with them and together they wandered Sanda's white beaches, they talked and laughed and had a wonderful time.

At Silversand Bay they ate a picnic lunch before rowing over to the Freshnish Isles in the dinghy. Mr McKinnon was fascinated by the Cave of the Echoes and all four of them held cupped hands to their mouths to shout "hallo-oo!" and "yoo-hoo!" till the resounding echoes rang in their ears and made them crackle.

Once back on Silversand Bay Mr McKinnon glanced up at a sturdy building known as Ard Cottage, sitting stark and grey on the headland. "That looks a lonely place," he commented. "There must be a marvellous view of the bay and the ocean from up there."

"That's Muckle's house," Jean told him. "He's a man who's lived here most of his life – except when he was at sea when he was younger. He can see everything from up there so don't be surprised if he's got his telescope on us right now, watching every move we make."

"Well, he can look all he likes; all I want is a bit of relaxation, so who votes we stow the dinghy and just lie about in the sun for a while? We've had a pretty energetic day so far."

The youngsters willingly fell in with his plans, glad just to laze about in the warm white sands after their labours with the oars.

Mr McKinnon lay back and put his hands behind his head.

"Dad," Kirsty said, "you're not going to sleep, are you? What about all those exciting things you had to tell us?"

He chuckled. "All right, I've kept you waiting long enough. Your mother and I have been to Donside to look at Red Rowans—"

'Red Rowans!" cried Kirsty.

'None other. We went through all the rooms,

just to see if it was feasible for Gran to have her own self-contained flat and if it was worth spending a lot of money doing the place up—"

"And?" Kirsty broke in, holding her breath.

Laughingly he pulled a strand of her hair. "Patience, Kirsty, patience. Your mother took a long time to come to a firm decision. She likes Paisley and—"

"That makes two of us," Andy said gruffly.

"And," went on Mr McKinnon forcibly, "she grumbled a bit about Red Rowans and all the work entailed in keeping the old house together until I drew out some plans of how it would look when modernised and it really fired her imagination – she can hardly wait to get there . . ."

"Great!" Kirsty couldn't contain herself. "When are we going?"

"We'll have to sell our own house first to get money to pay for everything so it's just a case of waiting for that. It isn't a good time to sell, we could wait long enough – but in the end – Red Rowans here we come."

"It sounds marvellous," Jean said, "Donside – Red Rowans."

"Oh, Jean, you would love it," Kirsty said with enthusiasm. "A little stream runs through the garden, there are woods and moors and purple hills in the distance. You'll have to come for holidays, we could have great times together, both on Sanda and in Donside."

The eyes of both girls sparkled; they saw the future stretching before them, rosy and bright. Only Andy was silent, moodily playing with the sand, letting it trickle through his fingers, not looking at anyone.

A shower of rain made them run to the shelter of the boat cave. Ten minutes later the sun started to appear again and with it came a rainbow, arching across the sky, embracing the rocks and distant islands in its brilliant hues.

"Look, Dad!" cried Kirsty, "isn't it the loveliest rainbow you ever saw? It's a sign of good luck."

He ruffled her hair. "Ay, sweetheart," he said softly, "I believe you're right at that."

Jean's gaze was far away as she watched the sky and softly she recited a verse by the Scottish poet, Iain Frank:

"Let us take hands,
And walk in the sands,
The waves lapping to and fro,
In the evening hour,
After a summer shower,
Let's look beyond the rainbow."

Mr McKinnon glanced at her. He liked Jean and he was glad that she and his daughter had befriended one another. But he sensed a sadness in her, even though she was always so smiling and vivacious. The poem she had just quoted was very poignant and somehow those green eyes of hers seemed indeed to be glimpsing something far beyond the rainbow. She and Kirsty had known great trauma in their young lives and as he remembered how worried he had been about his daughter a lump rose suddenly in his throat.

Holding out a hand to Jean, the other to Kirsty, he said, "Come on, the rain has stopped, we *will* walk in the sand and watch the waves lapping. Stop mooning about, Andy, take Jean's hand and let's *go!*"

Andy saw how happy his sister was, and making an effort he shrugged off his sulks and took the hand that Jean held out to him and they raced down the beach to the water's edge, yelling and laughing, quietness and sadness dissipating along with the rainbow that was now just a vestige of colour far off in the distance.

Before Mr McKinnon left next morning he folded Kirsty into his arms and hugged her so tightly she gave a yell of laughter and told him he was smothering her.

"I can't help it," he returned, holding her away to smile at her. "You looked as if you needed a good hug, and I seldom get the chance these days."

"All that will change soon, Dad," she said softly.

"Ay, Kirsty, the sooner the better. We'll all be a family again as we were before."

"Andy isn't too happy about us moving."

"I know, we'll have to give him time to get used to the idea and can only hope he'll come round in the end."

Andy appeared at that moment and Kirsty took her father's arm. "Come on, we'll walk you down to the harbour."

"I'm coming too." Jean had come in at Andy's back. "No show without Punch."

Mr McKinnon sailed away from Sanda with many fond farewells ringing in his ears. Kirsty and Andy stood side by side, watching him go, waving till the boat was just a speck in the distance.

"He's nice, your father," Jean said quietly. "I hope he comes back – bringing your mother with him next time."

"Thanks, Jean. A real family holiday, just like it used to be when we went to Donside to stay with Great-aunt Bella."

"I can't promise to be like Great-aunt Bella, her ways and mine might be just a wee bit different."

Kirsty's dimples showed and she put her head on one side and gave her friend a calculating glance. "Oh, I don't know, there are times when you seem at least a hundred years old."

Jean giggled. "Oh no, not yet, it'll take me till then to save up for that leather jacket I spoke about *and* I haven't had my head tattooed yet!"

They laughed and went off arm in arm, talking

about holidays, Andy following slowly in their wake.

"Andy's not quite himself," observed Jean. "He's been very quiet since your dad spoke about the move to Red Rowans."

"I know, I'll have to talk to him, appeal to his better nature."

Jean began to hum "Step We Gaily On We Go". Kirsty took up the song and they marched briskly along the road towards Croft an Cala, keeping time to the rhythm, their steps light though Jean was limping slightly as they approached the house.

"It's nothing, just a stone in my shoe," she said, proving her point by bending down to remove her shoe and give it a good shake.

"No wonder, it's got a hole in it," Kirsty pointed out.

"So it has, a good excuse to get a new pair. I fancy some of those Doc Martens. Just think, a hundred years from now, me in my leather jacket and a pair of Doc Martens as ancient as myself."

They laughed and went into the house in high spirits to get themselves ready to help Mr Anderson and the boys in the hayfields.

Chapter 14

The house was quiet. Mrs Anderson had gone to visit a friend in the village, Mr Anderson and the boys had gone out early to the fields and wouldn't be back till tea time; only Kirsty and Jean remained indoors.

"Just three days left of your holiday, Kirsty," Jean said as she gazed out of the window. "Let's make the most of them. What would you like to do? Your choice, it's a beautiful day."

"I'd love to go back to the Freshnish Isles one more time."

"The Freshnish Isles it is, just you and me together. We'll take Monty and Jeremy, save us walking. My legs are tired after all that tramping about we did yesterday."

"Only thing is," Kirsty made a face, "we'll never manage to drag the boat down to the water on our own."

"No need," said Jean triumphantly. "It's low tide, we can walk over, we'll be perfectly safe in the caves for at least an hour. Help me get a picnic packed, we can have our lunch on one of the islands."

Half an hour later they were ready to go. Jean left a note for her mother on the table, explaining what they had decided to do, telling her not to worry if they were back late since they would stay out as long as the weather held.

Monty and Jeremy were delighted to be included in the day's outing and they set off at a frisky pace, eager to get to the beach and the sea.

Kirsty had only ever seen the Freshnish Isles surrounded by water and it was a strange sensation for her to stand on Silversand Bay, gazing over the expanse of ridged sand and rocks that separated her from the Cave of the Echoes.

"It's only the high tides that make them into islands," explained Jean. "It's great fun to get to them either way, by boat or by foot. We'll leave the donkeys here – they would only be a nuisance inside the caves and might slip on the rocks."

The donkeys were tethered in a shady spot beside a small oasis of succulent grass and the girls set off, Kirsty carrying the picnic basket, Jean the jackets in case it rained. On the way over they kept their eyes open for interesting shells and between them gathered quite a few for Kirsty to take home.

The sun beat hotly down, the sea shimmered in the distance and Kirsty felt as if she were on the edge of the world and loved the feeling of space and light surrounding her.

It was cool inside the Cave of the Echoes, sun

flooded the entrance, the lagoon cast dancing reflections on the great vaulted roof. Kirsty couldn't resist a few "yoo-hoo's" and "hallo's" but both girls were hungry and it wasn't long before they were delving into the picnic basket.

"Let's sit on the rocks and dangle our feet in the pool," Jean suggested. "I'm not feeling energetic enough to go swimming."

They sat companionably side by side on a large rock, their feet in the clear sea water, discussing future plans.

"What would you like to do when you leave school?" Jean asked.

"Well, I used to think I'd like to be an air hostess but at least four other girls in my class want that too so I suppose it's just a phase."

"Why not a pilot? Girls do lots of things that men do nowadays. Think of how exciting that would be, and everything is computerised so you could just sit back and watch the world go by."

"All right, I'll be a pilot," Kirsty said with a laugh. "Only thing is, I'm not so good at maths and things like that though we do have computers in the classroom so at least that's one step in the right direction. How about you?"

Jean sat back, swinging her feet, her eyes gazing upwards. "Oh, I'm a very contented sort of person really and don't have many ambitions. Ideally I would love to stay on at An Cala and help Dad run the croft but one of the boys at least will likely get there before me. My second choice is to work with children who are deprived in one way or another."

"I wouldn't have the patience for that," Kirsty said with a grin. "I would get exasperated and fly off the handle too easily. Of course, we could always wait for those men that Meg saw in our cups – just sit around, looking good, twiddling our thumbs till they came and swept us off our feet . . . Oh, look . . .!"

She bent over to stare into the water. "Down there, fish, flounders I think, let's try and spear some. It would be a lovely surprise for your mother to have fresh fish to cook for dinner."

Jean caught her mood of enthusiasm and they went outside to look for a suitable piece of wood. That was easier said than done, however; the tides took away everything that had been washed up and for fully fifteen minutes they hunted amongst the rocks and even went into one of the smaller caves in their search.

"There's something." Kirsty pounced on a long slender tree branch, bleached white by sun and sea. "Just the thing, the end is nice and sharp and we'll make it even better with the knife you brought in the basket."

Before long they were sitting once more on the rocks, Kirsty poised ready with her "spear".

"Gotcha!" She made a lunge and came up with a silvery fish pinioned on the end of her stick. "I'm going in," she told Jean. "It's nice and shallow and I'll see the fish better."

Within half an hour she had caught three more fish. Jean was astounded. "You're a marvel. I thought you might be exaggerating a bit when you said you were as good as Hamish."

"Of course I'm as good!" Kirsty hooted indignantly. "My Dad wouldn't have stood for anything less than complete attention when he showed me how to spear *and* tickle the fish."

"All right, all right, I'm impressed,' Jean giggled. "I'm coming in too, I want to try my hand out."

So saying she slid off the rock and lowered herself gently into the water.

"Take the stick," directed Kirsty, "I'll show you what to do."

Jean was utterly entranced by the whole experience of wading about in the pool, staring down into the cool turquoise water, holding her breath every time a fish swam past her feet. "I feel like Neptune," she said in a hushed voice. "Too bad we haven't got a three-pronged trident, then we could get several at a time."

But despite all her attempts she failed to make a single catch. "How do you do it?" she asked Kirsty in frustration.

"Experience. The water deflects your aim so you have to make allowances. Look, I'll hold the stick with you and we'll try it together."

Three minutes later Jean landed her first flounder. "I did it!" she cried. "With a little help from my friend of course."

So absorbed were they in what they were doing they failed to notice the time till Jean looked up suddenly and saw that the sunlight was no longer slanting into the cave.

"Oh no!" she yelled, glancing at her watch. "We've been here for almost two hours!" Scrambling up on to the ledge she hurried to the entrance and saw that the tide was coming in fast, leaving only a narrow neck of land between the Freshnish Isles and Sanda.

"If we hurry we might make it!" she shouted, coming back in to collect her things. She stopped suddenly, her breath indrawn, then she collapsed and fell, her face contorted in pain.

"What is it?" Kirsty came running to Jean's side.

"I think I must have stumbled on a stone or something, my leg just gave way under me."

"Is it – your bad leg? The one that was operated on?"

"Yes, but don't worry. I've just twisted it, that's all. Help me up, we've got to try and get over before we're cut off altogether."

Kirsty held on to her while she pulled herself upright but with a groan she sank back. "Give me a minute – it's throbbing a bit and won't support me. Go and look outside and tell me what's happening."

Kirsty did as she was bid, coming back to report, "The water is swirling about but there's still a clear strip of sand big enough to walk on."

"Let's try again." Jean held up her hand and once more Kirsty took her weight. Jean managed a few steps before falling back exhausted. "It's no use, I can't do it, it just needs rest, that's all."

"You can make it if you put your arm round my shoulder," Kirsty said persuasively.

Jean shook her head. "No, we'd both drown. The tide comes in fast in the narrows, particularly if the sea bed is low-lying as it is here. We'd never do it with me crawling around on my hands and knees.'

Kirsty couldn't help smiling at the picture Jean's words presented but in the next moment she was serious again. "The water won't reach the ledges, will it?" she asked anxiously.

"Only during winter and the equinoxes. We'll be all right, all we have to do is wait here for the tide to turn."

Kirsty tried not to show how worried she was about Jean's leg. Instead she jumped down into the pool, soaked her hanky in sea water and brought it back dripping. "This will help the pain," she said, gently applying the wet hanky to the sore knee.

Jean's hand came out and gripped her friend's arm. "Thanks, Kirsty, you're a pal. I want you to promise me something. When we get back don't tell Mum about this, it would only worry her. I'll say I twisted my ankle on a rock. It isn't anything serious."

"Has it happened before?"

"Not like this, though it has been painful for a day or two. I've been running about too much lately. It's my own fault."

"No, mine, it's been a hectic holiday. I've loved it all."

Kirsty sat down and put an arm round Jean's shoulder. Together they gazed silently into the pool, watching the sea swishing into it, rising higher and higher.

"This place was always special to me," Jean said softly. "Now it will be even more so. I'll never come back here without thinking about you, Kirsty, and the wonderful times we spent with each other."

Kirsty looked around her and felt her eyes filling up. "You and me and rainbows, Jean. I'll remember this holiday for the rest of my life."

It was cold in the cave and Jean shivered. "Let's sing," she said. "Songs of the sea, of fishing boats and mermaids, and seals calling from the rocks. It might help to keep our minds off our worries."

"Mermaids," Kirsty's eyes shone. "That story Robbie told, Kalak Mar and the seal people, Vera so sad to leave her sweetheart behind."

"Perhaps a big romantic lad like Iain will come and rescue us," Jean laughed, forgetting her pain.

"Rescue us from the sea," Kirsty said dreamily, carried away by her friend's words. Then she smiled. "Just as long as he doesn't come on the back of a kelpie to lift us up and disappear with us down into the waves."

Jean began to sing and soon Kirsty joined in, their voices echoing all around the cave. And all the while the water rose higher, swelling the pool, silken green sea water that hushed and whispered and occasionally thudded against the rocks below.

Then quite unexpectedly a boat came shooting into the cave, like a cork from a bottle. In it bobbed a bright red head, next to it another wearing a green woollen cap over steel-grey hair.

Kirsty stood up. "Hamish!" she yelled. "And Muckle!"

The boat came nearer and Hamish jumped out, followed by Muckle who tied the rope to a spur of rock.

"Jean hurt her leg," Kirsty explained swiftly, more glad to see Hamish than she would ever admit. "How did you know we were here?"

"I was visiting Muckle at Ard Cottage," Hamish explained. "I looked from the window and saw you walking across the narrows. A good while later I looked again and saw the tide coming in and Jeremy and Monty still on the beach with no sign of you two . . . so . . . here we are."

He sounded very matter of fact but there was a flush on his cheeks when Kirsty gripped his arm and said simply, "Thanks, Hamish, it's so good to see you. We could have frozen to death in here."

Muckle took one look at Jean's strained face and without more ado he swept her up into his strong arms and placed her carefully in the boat. Kirsty was about to follow when she remembered something. "My fish!" she exclaimed and rushed away to collect her precious flounders.

"You caught those?" Hamish asked.

Kirsty's nod was nonchalant. "I speared them."

Hamish's face was a study of surprise. "You *speared* them?"

"Yes, all except one, Jean got that."

He looked hurt. "I was going to teach you, I was coming along tonight to ask if you were free tomorrow."

Her heart melted. "Dad taught me a little bit. I'm not nearly as good as you though. You got yours when the tide was in, today the pool was so shallow I could practically scoop them out with my hand . . . and I'd like nothing better than to come with you tomorrow."

The boat glided out of the cave and halfway over to Sanda Hamish's hand crept into Kirsty's. She felt comforted by his touch and though he said nothing his eyes were shining.

"Kalak Mar," Jean murmured, "Vera and Iain."

"What was that, Jean?" questioned Hamish.

"Nothing, just thinking aloud."

Kirsty caught her eye. They smiled at one another as they remembered the legend of the seal people.

Mrs Anderson looked worried when Muckle carried in her daughter until Jean reassured her that she was suffering from nothing more than a twisted ankle.

"How strange," Mrs Anderson said as Muckle deposited Jean carefully on the couch. "History repeats itself, Muckle McPhee."

Jean looked from one face to the other and saw that a stain of red had diffused Muckle's nut-brown cheeks.

"Is there some sort of secret between you two?" Jean asked curiously.

Mrs Anderson and Muckle eyed one another.

"I don't need to tell you about Muckle's Anchor, Jean," said her mother, "you know all there is to know about that. The little girl trapped under that anchor long ago was me. All I can remember was the tide coming in and the next thing I knew I was looking up into Muckle's handsome face as he carried me into the house. Seeing him bringing you in brought it all flooding back."

"It's a lovely story," said Jean surprised. "I wish I'd heard it sooner."

"Muckle wanted to forget all the fuss, he's that kind of man, modest to a fault."

An embarrassed-looking Muckle was standing

in the middle of the floor, twisting his cap in his hand, his face still as red as a beetroot. What Jean didn't know and never would was how he had fallen in love with her mother as she grew from a girl into a woman. But she had married Alan Anderson without ever knowing of Muckle's devotion to her. Sometimes he suspected that she guessed, especially as he had never married, and him so popular with the womenfolk who passed his way.

"Thanks for bringing Jean home," Mrs Anderson said softly.

"Yes, thank you, Muckle," echoed Jean.

"Think nothing of it," he said gruffly. "Let's just say I enjoy rescuing young maidens in distress, and of course, Hamish did his share. If it hadn't been for his sharp eyes – not to mention a curiosity as big as my own – you might be in that cave yet, Jean. I'll look in later to see how you are, lass. Right now I must be getting along."

He went quickly away and Mrs Anderson eyed her daughter. "Are you sure you're all right, Jean? You look pale."

"I'm fine, Mum, really. I tripped on a stone and my ankle went over. An hour or so of lazing about is all I need."

She was glad that Kirsty and Hamish came in just then, looking hot and dishevelled.

"I'll get us all a cup of tea." Mrs Anderson went off to the kitchen.

"Thanks for everything you two," Jean said

gratefully, "I don't know what I would have done without you."

"Think nothing of it," Hamish said modestly. "It was strange . . . when Muckle and me were coming over in the boat I kept thinking of Kalak Mar and the seal people."

"Really?" Jean said faintly, not daring to look at Kirsty.

"I remembered Vera and Iain and how they disappeared into the sea and I didn't want that to happen to you or Kirsty. Strange things do happen on the islands, you know," he ended mysteriously.

"Yes, I know they do," Jean said with a straight face.

Hamish glanced at Kirsty. "Don't you think so, Kirsty?"

"Well, I've never been rescued from a cave before."

"That's what I mean," he said earnestly. "I looked from that window and it was as if – as if I heard your voice – calling me."

"The call of the islands," said Jean.

"The call of the sea," said Kirsty.

"The call of the mermaids," said Hamish.

The arrival of Mrs Anderson with the tea brought the children back to earth though a feeling of magic remained with them long after the last bun had been eaten, and the last drop of tea drunk.

Chapter 15

The holiday was over all too soon. It was a morning of light summer showers but bright for all that, the sun glinting on the sea, the beaches dazzling white, the larks singing high in the sky. Kirsty felt a lump rising in her throat as she stood at the door, breathing in the salt-laden air.

Jean came quietly out of the house and taking Kirsty's hand she murmured the words of Iain Frank's poem:

> "Let us take hands,
> And walk in the white sands,
> The waves lapping to and fro
> In the evening hour,
> After a summer shower,
> Let's look beyond the rainbow."

Kirsty fumbled for her hanky. "Oh, Jean," she said shakily. "I think I'm going to cry."

"Don't worry about me," Jean said softly. "I spent a good part of last night crying my eyes out. I'm going to miss you, Kirsty, it's been wonderful having you here."

Tearfully they gazed at one another. "I'll be back," Kirsty said in a wobbly sort of voice. "We *will* walk in the sands together and look at beautiful rainbows in the sky."

"Yes," replied Jean with a watery sniff, "we'll do that, Kirsty – and remember – we are for ever going to be."

"And when we're feeling down we'll think of that little verse Meg told us about polishing up the dark side."

Jean took her friend's arm. "Come and say goodbye to Mum and Dad and the boys."

"The house will be dead without you," Mrs Anderson told Andy and Kirsty.

"You'll be back, people always come back to Sanda." Mr Anderson gave each of them a firm handshake before going out to where the tractor was sputtering noisily.

"Ay, you must come back," Jim said with one of his devilish grins. "You were a good help in the fields and earned your keep. Glad you learned to drive the tractor, Andy, it saved me a lot of time."

"Och, don't listen to him." Robbie's brown eyes glinted. "He always says the wrong things. Next time, Kirsty, I'll show you how to drive the tractor so that you'll become as good as Andy."

"She'll likely be better," put in Jean with a wink at her friend.

"We'll come down to the harbour to see you

off." Jim was already halfway upstairs to fetch his bagpipes.

Kirsty saw a rainbow as she and Andy were leaving Croft an Cala for the first stage of their journey home. It was a big rainbow, encompassing all the little green and blue islands that shimmered like jewels on the horizon, with the Freshnish Isles caught in the dazzling hues.

"Look, Andy." Kirsty held her breath. "It's as if it appeared specially for us."

They both stared entranced, drinking in their fill of it, knowing it could disappear at any time – there one moment – gone the next.

And then a strange thing happened. They saw Jean, caught as it were, in the shimmering colours. She had just come out of the house and somehow she was there inside the rainbow, a half-real figure touched by the brilliance and light.

"How odd," breathed Kirsty. "She's part of it all, part of the sky and the sea and the rainbow."

The experience shook Kirsty. She wondered what it all meant, if it was a sign of something, something that she didn't understand yet but would in days to come.

Jean came running towards them and suddenly everything was normal again, the rainbow vanished, the islands and the ocean were as they had been before, and Jean was Jean, with nothing different about her at all. The boys appeared and together they all walked down to the harbour where the ferry was just tying up.

Muckle arrived to seek out the children and say his goodbyes. For quite some minutes there was a babble of voices as the islanders said their farewells to departing visitors.

Kirsty and Jean briefly embraced, too filled up with the poignancy of the moment to be able to say the things that were in their hearts.

"This is for you." Jean handed Kirsty a seal-shaped stone she had found on the beach long ago. "It will remind you of Kalak Mar and the seal people and you will remember Sanda every time you look at it."

"It's lovely." Kirsty gazed at the stone, the tears springing once more to her eyes. "But I don't need to be reminded of Sanda. I'll never forget it nor will I forget how good you and your family were to Andy and me."

The captain's voice came over the tannoy, reminding everyone that the steamer would be sailing in a few minutes and it was time for "all aboard". Kirsty followed Andy up the gangplank but she kept looking over her shoulder for a sign of Hamish who had promised to come to the harbour to see them off.

She had spent an energetic afternoon with him, spearing fish in a deep pool amongst the rocks of Silversand Bay, and afterwards they had walked up to the headland to have tea with Muckle at Ard Cottage.

"I wish you were staying longer," Hamish had said to Kirsty afterwards. "You and me like the same sort of things."

"There's always the next time," Kirsty had said, an affection in her for this boy whose resilient spirit had helped him to accept the death of both his parents. She knew, however, that he felt his loss keenly because he spoke about them sometimes as if they were still alive.

"I never used to think about death, Kirsty," he had confided. "Now I know what it's like to come up against it and that's why I understand how you and Jean must have felt when you were so ill." He had taken her hand at that point and held it firmly if briefly. In those moments she had known that there was more than just physical strength in Hamish Grant and that was why she watched for him so anxiously as she was about to leave Sanda far behind.

Then she saw his unmistakable red head coming along in the distance and she waited for him, quietly pleased that he hadn't forgotten.

"Sorry to be late," he called rather breathlessly. "I was doing some chores for Gran." Putting his hand in his pocket he withdrew a little enamel brooch in the shape of a rainbow. "I know how much you like rainbows," he told Kirsty as he handed it to her. "I saw this in the

147

village shop . . ." He grinned. "It was in my price range so I bought it for you. Think of me sometimes when you wear it."

"Oh, Hamish." Kirsty was so touched by his thoughtfulness she leaned forward and bestowed a kiss on his cheek. "Of course I'll think of you and hope we'll meet again one day."

Hamish blushed and consumed with shyness he turned away to push something into Andy's hand. "This is for you, I made it myself." It was a little flute, fashioned out of an elder branch, and Andy immediately put it to his lips to produce a few haunting notes.

The boat's engine was making busy noises and brother and sister could delay no longer. Moments later they were at the rails. Jim struck up on the bagpipes, playing "Will Ye No Come Back Again".

The ferry began to move away and Kirsty and Andy gazed down at all the faces that had become familiar and dear to them.

"It was a great holiday," Andy said quietly. "It would be good to come back someday."

Kirsty saw "Muckle's Anchor" in the bay where it had lain unmoved after so many years. In confidence Jean had told her the story about Muckle's rescue of her mother and it all came flooding back to Kirsty in those moments. "Yes, we'll come back, Andy," she murmured. "It's such a magical place, so many lovely things happen here."

"Let's go and get something to eat," he moved away from the rail. "I'm starving."

"But you've only just had breakfast. You're always hungry."

He gave her a quizzical look. "I thought that was normal."

"It is for you," she laughed.

He made tracks for the cafeteria but Kirsty lingered on deck, gazing at the island. It was receding rapidly into the distance, spanned by a large rainbow that held the hills and the houses and the people in its transient embrace.

PART THREE

Beyond the Rainbow

Chapter 16

It was strange going home to the busy streets of Paisley after the wide open spaces of Sanda. Kirsty wondered how she was going to be able to put up with it till she remembered that the house was up for sale and that some day – soon she hoped – they would all be living in Donside.

Mrs McKinnon welcomed them home with open arms and was eager to hear all their news.

"We brought you this." Andy handed his mother a box made of seashells. "It was hand-made on Sanda," he explained. "The kids collect the shells and the grown-ups make the boxes during the winter. We got one for Gran and Dad as well only his is smaller for cufflinks and tie-pins. It plays 'The Skye Boat Song'."

"How lovely." Mrs McKinnon opened her box and the notes of "The Mingulay Boat Song" tinkled out.

"Can we take Gran her box tomorrow?" asked Kirsty.

Mrs McKinnon laughed. "We wouldn't dare not to, she's been missing you and she wants to talk to you about Red Rowans."

Over tea the children told their mother about the things they had done and seen on Sanda and about the people they had met. "Muckle was interesting," said Andy, "he told us all about the things that had happened to him when he was at sea."

"Then there was Hamish." Kirsty glanced down at the rainbow brooch pinned to her blouse. "He gave me this."

"Oh, what a pretty brooch," said Mrs McKinnon. "He must have taken a liking to you, Kirsty."

"We had a lot in common," said Kirsty, flushing a little. She tried to hide her flaming cheeks in her teacup. "He only wanted to show me how to spear fish and play football."

Mrs McKinnon looked at her daughter in some surprise. "But, Kirsty, you already knew how to do these things before you went to Sanda . . ." She smiled. "Oh, I see, you pretended you couldn't because . . ."

"She wanted him to think she was helpless!" Andy said with a grin.

He ducked to avoid the cushion Kirsty aimed at his head.

Later, when the table was cleared and the dishes done they all sat round the fire talking.

"Dad enjoyed his visit to Sanda," said Mrs McKinnon. "He couldn't wait to tell you about Red Rowans." She glanced at Andy. "You're the only one who isn't keen on the move and I can understand perfectly how you feel since I felt exactly the same until I went to Donside. Somehow, seeing the old house brought all those happy holidays flooding back. Even so I wasn't convinced that moving there would work till Dad drew out some plans and made me see how it could look when the alterations were done."

"Aren't you excited – just a little bit?" Kirsty asked her brother.

"Apprehensive would be a better description," he said cautiously. "I'm trying to get used to the idea so don't try to complicate matters by expecting me to say things I don't feel."

"Sleep on it," advised his mother, "and go on sleeping on it till you feel better about it."

The grandfather clock was ticking loudly in the hall as Kirsty passed it on her way to bed. It was a familiar sound, one that seemed to follow her into her room and keep time to her movements as she prepared for bed. Carefully she placed her little seal stone on her bedside cabinet where she could see it as soon as she wakened. She snuggled under the quilt, remembering Jean and all those other lovely people she had met on holiday.

The door creaked open and Chanter came into the room. Jumping on to the bed he curled into a ball and buried his nose in his tail.

"You know what Mum said," Kirsty whispered. "You shouldn't be up here, she'll throw you out if she sees you."

Chanter purred loudly and yawned and Kirsty giggled and ruffled his fur.

The notes of "The Mingulay Boat Song" filtered through from the living room. Kirsty knew that her mother was enjoying a few minutes of peace by the fire, perhaps thinking about Donside and Red Rowans. Kirsty reached out for her seal stone and held it tightly in her hand. It felt warm, as if it were alive.

"I know you'll bring us luck," she whispered. "I also think you have magic in you. If so I want you to help Andy feel happy about moving. He must surely like the idea of being able to ask Jean and Robbie and Jim to come and spend a holiday with us – Hamish too of course . . ." She smiled to herself. "It wouldn't be the same without him."

The seal stone fitted nicely into the palm of her hand and was now so warm it seemed as if it were really breathing.

Sleep stole over her but she never let go of her seal stone. That stayed with her the whole night long and was even there in her dreams of Sanda with its seas and its rainbows.

Chapter 17

More than a month had gone by and the flat still hadn't been sold. In fact no one had shown much interest in it and the family were growing more despondent with each passing day.

"It wasn't meant to be," Andy commented, rather smugly, Kirsty thought.

"That's enough, Andy!" Bob McKinnon told his son sharply. "It's just a bad time to sell, that's all. You should stop behaving so selfishly and start to think of others for a change!"

Andy reddened. "I didn't mean it," he muttered and took himself smartly out of the room.

"Bob," Mrs McKinnon gave her husband a reproachful look, "arguing isn't going to help matters."

"Then you should have thought of that sooner!" he returned irritably. "If we had tried to sell the house in the spring we might have had it off our hands by now! As it is we could wait for ever the way the country stands at the moment."

"So, you're blaming me!" Mrs McKinnon's temper flared. "The reason we're trying to sell the house at all is because of your stubbornness not to leave that job in Aberdeen."

"We've been through all this, Jan," he said warningly. "I hope you're not going to rake it all up again."

Kirsty hoped so too. She gazed from one blazing face to the other and with a sigh she too left the room.

Two evenings later the phone rang. When Mrs McKinnon went to answer it the voice of the sheltered housing warden came over the line.

"Mrs McKinnon? I'm sorry but I'm afraid your mother's had a heart attack and has been taken to hospital."

"Oh . . ." Mrs McKinnon's voice was blank with shock. "I'll go there right away, it must have been all the excitement. She's been anxious lately about the move to Donside."

"Yes, she has been rather keyed up but she's a hardy soul, Mrs McKinnon, and I'm sure she'll pull through all right."

Mrs McKinnon thanked the warden and put the phone down. The family had heard snatches of the conversation and they were waiting with sober faces to hear the rest.

"Mother has had a heart attack." Mrs McKinnon's eyes were dazed, her voice was trembling. "She's in hospital, I'll have to go there at once."

"I'll come with you." Bob McKinnon put his arm round his wife's shoulders. "Don't worry, she's tough is your mother, she'll fight like the devil to get over this."

"Thank heaven you're here, Bob," his wife told him. "I don't know what I would have done if I'd been on my own."

Andy and Kirsty were watching their mother, their faces white. "You wouldn't have been on your own with us here." Andy was the first to speak, his voice firm. "We'll manage fine till you and Dad get back."

Kirsty went into the hall and returned with her mother's jacket. "Poor Gran," she whispered, "she was so happy about everything. I wish I could come with you, Mum."

They rushed away, leaving Andy and Kirsty to gaze at one another. "We'd better see to the tea." He said the first thing that came into his head.

"Is that all you can think about?" she tossed at him. "Your stomach as usual!"

"No, it isn't all, and stop shouting. You've been like a little wildcat this while back, snapping at people, mooning about. Are you feeling ill again? Is that it?"

She turned away. How could she tell him that he was nearer the truth than he knew. She *had* been feeling unwell lately and that in turn had made her bad-tempered.

"Kirsty." Suddenly he was beside her, his breath fanning her ear. "You aren't hiding anything, are you?"

For a moment she was tempted to confide in him. Then she remembered Granny Reid and the terrible thing that had happened to her. How could she burden her family with more problems at a time like this . . .? "It's nothing, Andy," she lied, "I must be catching a cold, that's all. I've got a headache and think I'll lie down for a while."

"Aren't you going to have any tea?"

"No, I'm not hungry, you have yours."

"But I can't eat a whole casserole all to myself."

She managed to smile at him and say cheekily, "Can't you? You could have fooled me, Andy McKinnon. Leave a bit, I might be able to eat it later. If not give it to Chanter."

It was midnight when Mr and Mrs McKinnon got home. Kirsty heard them coming in and went through to the living room where Andy had fallen asleep in front of the television.

He struggled awake, however, when Kirsty gave him a shake. Wordlessly they stared at their parents, waiting for them to speak.

"Gran has stabilised," their father told them. "She's in intensive care on a heart monitor but she was able to speak to us and even managed to sound a bit bossy."

His wife gave a shaky laugh. "Och, Bob, you are the limit – but it's true . . ." She turned to the children. "Your gran always was a tough old bird. My father used to say you could pluck her and boil her and she would still pop up smiling."

Andy and Kirsty breathed sighs of relief which waned a little when their father added, "Tough or no, she *has* had a heart attack and the next few days will be crucial for her so we'll all have to pray that she gets well again."

"I'll make a cup of tea." Kirsty went to put the kettle on, glad to be alone for a moment. Her legs felt weak and she sat down on a kitchen stool, her thoughts on her gran. Oh, I *will* pray for you, Gran, she thought.

Her cheeks were wet and putting a hand up to her eyes she dashed the tears away. She had to be strong, more than ever she had to be strong, for everyone's sake as well as her own.

The hospital phoned next morning to say that Mrs Reid was not out of danger but that her condition was remaining stable.

"Thank goodness." Mrs McKinnon put the phone down and almost stumbled over Kirsty at her back. "Kirsty! Still listening at doors! This time I don't blame you but the news about Gran is hopeful, she's bearing up well . . ." She paused and studied her daughter more closely. "I'm not so sure I can say the same about you, you're very pale. Do you feel all right?"

"Well, I've got a cold and I'm worried about Gran. Are you going to see her today?"

"Yes, Dad phoned his work and has managed

to get some time off so he'll be coming with me. He'll be on holiday next week anyway so it won't be so bad with him around. Before I go I have a few things to see to. You'd better get ready for school. You'll be late but when you explain to your teacher the reasons why I'm sure she'll understand."

Kirsty went to the window to look along the street, hoping to catch the postman before she went to school. Ever since the holiday on Sanda she and Jean had regularly exchanged letters. Almost a fortnight had passed, however, with no word from Jean, and Kirsty was beginning to wonder if everything was all right.

A yawn escaped her as she stood there. She felt heavy with weariness and could easily have stayed in bed that morning but that would have aroused everyone's suspicions. Somehow she had to keep going. Her parents had enough to cope with just now without adding to their difficulties.

At that moment the postman came along, head bent against the driving rain. Kirsty was at the door to meet him, wishing him good morning and asking if he had anything for her.

"Is it love letters you're after?" he said with a wink which made her wish he wasn't such a nosy postman. It was almost as if he knew that Hamish had written to her once or twice, each time enclosing a little wild flower from Sanda.

"Mostly for your mother." The postman was flicking through the letters. "Never mind, you might get something tomorrow." He handed her the mail and with a parting wink he went on his way with a cheery whistle on his lips.

Mrs McKinnon glanced through the letters: nothing much, circulars, a bill, then she paused as she came to an envelope bearing the official hospital stamp. Tearing it open she read it quickly. "It's from the hospital, Kirsty." She raised her voice and Kirsty came through from her room. "Dr Kominski wants you at his clinic for a checkup. It's just routine, making sure that everything is all right."

Kirsty turned a dismayed face. "The hospital?" She couldn't keep a wobble from her voice. "But I saw the doctor when I came home from Sanda. I don't need to see him again."

"He has to keep an eye on you, Kirsty, you know that as well as I do."

Andy came through from his room, yawning and bleary-eyed. His tie was squinty, his hair standing on end. "Did I hear something about the hospital? Is it about Gran?"

"No, the hospital phoned. Gran still isn't out of danger but she's bearing up well. A letter just came from the infirmary wanting Kirsty at the clinic for a checkup . . ." Mrs McKinnon broke off to glare at her son. "Just look at you, anyone would think you'd been dragged through a hedge backwards! Right . . ." she took him by the

163

shoulder, "you can make your way back to your room and tidy yourself up properly. It's high time you took some pride in your appearance! I don't want to see you again till you've made yourself presentable. Thank goodness your father will be home on holiday in a few days, he might see then what I have to contend with every morning of the week!"

Kirsty's shoulders sagged as she listened to Dr Kominski. It was her second time back at the clinic in a week and he was telling her that her blood count was below normal. That meant she would have to be admitted to hospital.

"I'm sorry about this, Kirsty," he said gently. "I had hoped you would stay in remission longer, perhaps even for good but it looks as if the leukaemia has come back and this time we'll have to administer stronger drugs in higher doses. It's always harder to fight leukaemia the second time around."

Mrs McKinnon heard all this in a state of disbelief. She had truly imagined that her daughter would get the all clear. Certainly she had been suffering from a bad head cold and had lost both her colour and her appetite, symptoms which Kirsty herself had attributed to her cold.

Mrs McKinnon said all this to Doctor Kominski who nodded in understanding. "That's how it works. Everything seems to be fine and going along well then BAM!, it strikes. And perhaps . . ." here he turned to look at Kirsty, "you haven't been telling anyone about how you've really been feeling?"

Kirsty had been staring out the window all the time the doctor was speaking to her mother. His voice seemed to drone on with all that technical stuff about her illness. Outside there was a motorway, above it was a steeply inclined fly-over, on it the cars were coming down, one after the other in an endless procession. Just like little bubbles in a straw – just like the "Lukes" in her blood, on and on – for ever!

She slumped in her chair; gently her mother took her hand. "You've fought and won before, Kirsty, you can do it again. I'll be with you all the way – and so will Dad."

Kirsty looked up. "Mum, I might die this time!" Her voice rose. "Do you hear me! I might die! It was bad enough before but now the treatment will be worse. Dr Kominski said so himself."

He nodded. "There will be hefty doses of chemotherapy, Kirsty, and I'm not going to lie and say that you won't go through some bad spells. But as I said before, everyone reacts differently; you might be one of the lucky ones and escape the worst after effects of the treatment."

Kirsty suddenly felt a hundred years old. "Lucky!" she said bitterly. "What's lucky about getting leukaemia in the first place? Why did it have to be me anyway?"

"Kirsty," with tears in her eyes Mrs McKinnon helped her daughter to her feet, "we have to go home. I'll need to visit Gran and we must get your things packed."

"Gran – yes – poor Gran." Kirsty spoke in a strange, far-away voice. "Don't tell her about me, Mum, not just yet, not till she's better."

"That's my Kirsty," Mrs McKinnon said huskily and led her daughter away.

As soon as they got home and had broken the news Kirsty went to her father. His arms were strong and warm and comforting. "There, there, sweetheart," he soothed, stroking her hair with gentle hands, "we're all going to be in this with you, helping you to fight it. You'll give it all you've got, I know you will, you're not our lass for nothing. You've got my stubbornness and your mother's determination – not forgetting Gran's contribution of toughness. So you've got some mighty powerful forces working for you."

Kirsty raised a tear-stained face. "It's easy to say these things, Dad, but I don't feel very strong or tough. I'm afraid, more even than the last time because now I know what it's all about."

Andy appeared at that moment, strained and apprehensive-looking. "Kirsty . . ." He spoke his sister's name dully. "I'm sorry – I don't know what to say." Turning on his heel he went off to his room and his father shook his head.

"All of this has been a big shock for Andy,

sweetheart. He's at sixes and sevens and doesn't really know how to handle the situation. That's why he's been so grumpy all summer. I know him, he's bottling it all up, trying hard to be a man for your sake."

Kirsty's face softened. "I know that, Dad, boys of his age are like that. They don't want anybody to think they're soft so they have to hide their true feelings."

Bob McKinnon gazed at his daughter. "Words of wisdom from the mouth of a babe. You've grown up this year, Kirsty."

He smiled at her but his eyes were sad.

Chapter 18

Kirsty was packing the things she would need for the hospital when the phone went. Her mother had offered to help but Kirsty had refused, wanting to be alone for a while. She seemed to have done nothing but cry since her visit to the clinic that morning and now she felt drained and exhausted.

"I'll get it." Mrs McKinnon was already in the hall, gingerly picking up the phone, a dread in her that this might be bad news about her mother.

But the call had nothing to do with Granny Reid; it was Mrs Anderson calling from Sanda and the news she had to tell Kirsty's mother was anything but good. When at last Mrs McKinnon put down the phone she stood for a long time beside the hall table, her fingers to her mouth, a frown of despair creasing her brow.

When she finally moved it was to her husband she went. "Oh, Bob," she whispered, "that was Mrs Anderson phoning about Jean. She's back in hospital and she's very ill; she's had surgery on her leg but it hasn't done much good, now the cancer is through her body – and there's little hope of her recovery. I can't – I simply can't tell Kirsty after what she's been through today."

"Jan," Bob McKinnon took his wife's hand, "she'll have to know. Think about it. She's going back into hospital, to the same ward she was in before. Jean will be there and imagine the shock Kirsty would get not knowing beforehand."

"Oh," Jan McKinnon shook her head. "I hadn't thought of that . . ." She stared at him with horror in her eyes. "What's happening to us, Bob? First Mother, then Kirsty – and now – this."

"Steady on, Jan." He put his arms round her. "We can't let go for Kirsty's sake, she's going to need all the support she can get. We'll go through and tell her together. Where's Andy?"

"Out – at some football match with a friend."

"Maybe just as well, he too has had enough for one day. Let's go through and get it over with." She hesitated and he gave her a gentle little shake. "Come on, where's that determination of character I know so well? I need to feel your strength, Jan, because if truth be known I'm just as stunned by all this as you are."

Kirsty heard them out in silence. When they had finished speaking she sank on to the bed, her eyes big and dark in her horrified face. "No," she protested, "not Jean as well! I can't stand it! I can't stand it! Why is all this happening? We were so happy, now it's all been taken away."

Putting her hands to her face she gave way to great heart-rending sobs while her parents held her, letting her tears wash away some of her tension.

"Kirsty," Mrs McKinnon stroked the hair from her daughter's hot face, "you're going to need an awful lot of courage for what lies ahead – and you're going to need it for more than just yourself. Jean must be in a dreadful state of anxiety. You and she have shared so much these past months; she's your best friend, Kirsty, and you're going to need one another very much."

Kirsty scrubbed her eyes with her father's hanky then her head went up. "I know, Mum, just give me a minute, please. I knew something was wrong when Jean didn't write but I never thought it would be this bad. When I thought I was taking ill again I didn't say anything either – I was scared and I knew how upset you were about Gran – so I said nothing." She looked at them, "Now maybe I've left it too late."

"No, Kirsty." Her father spoke firmly. "It isn't too late, it's never too late to fight for what you believe in and you have to have faith in yourself above all else."

"Ay, Dad," she said quietly and squeezed his hand.

Kirsty didn't know how she was going to face Jean, never mind cope with her own feelings. It was terrible to be coming back to her old ward;

she had almost forgotten the antiseptic smells and the feeling of illness everywhere.

She followed Nurse Bradley up the ward. "I've put you beside Jean, Kirsty." Nurse Bradley stopped at a cubicle halfway up the ward and placed Kirsty's little case on a chair. "I knew you would want to be beside her, you always got on so well."

Kirsty's stomach was churning, she hardly dared look at the bed next to hers but Jean was asleep; nothing could be seen of her except her fair hair spreading over the pillow.

The curtains were whipped round Kirsty. For the next half-hour the nurses came and went and then Dr Kominski with two other doctors. Kirsty thought the bustle would never stop but at last Nurse Bradley pulled back the curtains and Kirsty was at last alone.

Jean was awake, a very different Jean from the one that Kirsty remembered. Her face had lost its fullness, there were dark smudges under her eyes – and she was thin – much too thin.

"Oh, Jean," Kirsty whispered. "I've been longing to see you again but not – like this – in hospital again – after all the lovely times we had on Sanda."

They stared at one another, each with tears in their eyes. Jean's hand came out but she was too weak to span the gap between the beds. Kirsty couldn't bear it, she got up and went to Jean to put her arms round her. They cried together, saying nothing, their hearts too full to put what they felt into words.

"You know your mum phoned mine?" Kirsty said eventually, wiping her streaming eyes. "I couldn't believe it – so much else had happened, first my gran taking ill, then me. Hearing about you was the last straw somehow."

"I know," nodded Jean. "I felt the same when Sister said you were coming back in and that you knew about me. I couldn't write to you, Kirsty, everything happened so quickly in the end. After I hurt my leg that time in the cave I was limping about and Mum took me to see my doctor who sent me here. I got home after the op to my leg then I started coughing and feeling breathless and I was whipped back in."

"I've been feeling bad for a week or so," admitted Kirsty. "I didn't tell anyone because my gran had a heart attack and my folks had enough worry and running about – also, Jean, I was frightened. I didn't want to believe my leukaemia was back so I kept quiet about it. At the clinic Doc Kominski took some blood tests and when I went back for the results he said I was to come into hospital right away . . ."

She took something from her pocket and held it up for Jean to see. It was a photograph of them both perched on the rocks on the beach, smiling and happy; behind them was Croft an Cala, spanned by an enormous rainbow. "It was the only one of the holiday snaps to come out." Kirsty spoke slowly, gazing at the picture. "The camera was letting in light and none of the others turned out but it doesn't matter, as long as we have this one."

Jean took the picture and stared at it for a long time. "So happy," she said softly, "something to remember always. I don't think I'll be seeing any more of my island rainbows, but at least we've got this."

"You'll always see rainbows, Jean, wherever you go, and remember what Meg said? 'If no bright side you can see, then polish up the dark side.' "

"Meg . . ." Jean's voice shook. "I wish she was here now to cheer us up with her courage." The girls looked over to the bed that used to be Meg's.

Kirsty placed the photo on Jean's cabinet. "We'll look at this instead and think of Sanda and how bright it all was."

As Kirsty's parents came walking up the ward to say goodbye to their daughter, Mrs McKinnon's heart turned over at the sight of the two girls comforting one another, such good friends – right from the beginning. She touched Jean's hand. "Jean, Kirsty has spoken about you so much since her holiday on Sanda. Too bad you had to meet again like this . . ."

She hesitated, at a loss for words, and her husband stepped in to fill the gap. "You two will have to buck one another up. It won't be easy but at least you have one another."

Jean nodded. "I know, Kirsty was always good for me."

"You were good for each other," Mrs McKinnon said and gave both girls a hug.

Goodbyes were said and as Kirsty watched her parents walking away her heart cried out to go with them. She turned back to Jean. "Mum's right about one thing, it is awful to meet again like this – but at least we're together again."

Jean smiled wanly. "Together again," she whispered and was asleep before Nurse Bradley came up the ward to chase Kirsty back to her own bed.

Chapter 19

It was Kirsty's third time in hospital in a month. Nurse Bradley finished taking her blood pressure and folded away the stethoscope.

"How are you feeling, Kirsty?" she asked in her kindly way.

"Terrible," Kirsty admitted frankly, "worse than before. I have to rest all the time."

"Jean has been missing you," Nurse Bradley said, plumping the pillows at Kirsty's back and helping her to sit up. "Visiting time soon, I'll get out your brush and comb so that you can make yourself beautiful."

Kirsty shrank back as if she had been struck. "How can I? I don't have any hair! A duster and some polish would be better than a brush and comb!"

Nurse Bradley looked at Kirsty's head. All her lovely hair had gone and the medication and treatment she had received had made her ill and sick.

Jean was also very ill. Every time Kirsty was readmitted to the ward she saw drastic changes in her friend; she was small and frail-looking in the hospital bed but her strength of character had somehow kept her going. Her lungs had been affected by her illness and she had to have oxygen when it became too painful for her to breathe.

Even so she still managed to see the lighter side of life and at Kirsty's words she smiled. "Don't take it to heart, Kirsty, we're all baldies together! I thought I would have to wait till I was a hundred before this happened. Now look at me! I don't suppose you could arrange to have my head tattooed, Nurse Bradley?"

"No, but I can comb your wigs for you and make them look as natural as possible." She retrieved the wigs from the respective lockers and deftly brushed them into shape. "There you are. Just let me put them on for you and you'll be beautiful in no time."

"I look like a Barbie doll." Jean gazed at herself in the mirror that Nurse Bradley held up for her before sinking back on her pillows, as if the effort of holding up her head had been too much for her.

"And I look just like Diana Ross." Kirsty tried to sound light-hearted but couldn't help feeling dreadfully self-conscious about her appearance.

"Nothing matters except that you get well again," her father had told her. "Your hair will grow back, right now you're in the height of fashion. A lot of people wear wigs these days and you look a million dollars in yours." After that she had tried to accept the way she looked – as Jean had done. Jean wore her wig without fuss; she accepted a lot of things without fuss and Kirsty tried to follow her example with as much spirit as she could.

A few minutes later the doors opened and the visitors came streaming up the ward. Mr and Mrs Anderson, Robbie and Jim were first to arrive, followed by Mr and Mrs McKinnon and Andy.

Jean's eyes lit up. "Mum! Dad! Robbie! Jim! What are you all doing here? All the way from Sanda!"

Mrs Anderson put her arms round her daughter and held her close as she explained. "We're staying with Kirsty's mum, she offered to put us up for a few days." Mrs Anderson didn't tell Jean that the hospital had requested that all the family be near at hand over the next few days as Jean was growing weaker with each passing hour.

"We've got another surprise for you." Robbie tried to speak cheerfully, but his smile never reached his eyes. He had last seen his sister a week ago and even in that short time she had become thinner and her skin looked transparent. "He's coming up the ward now."

At that, Hamish Grant came marching up the ward, wearing his Sunday best suit, his spiky red hair brushed into shining obedience. "My gran let me come with the Andersons." He spoke quietly, his eyes going first to Jean and then to

Kirsty, nothing in his tone giving away the sadness he felt at seeing how ill they both looked. A vision came to him, of Jean on Monty's broad back, her laughter ringing out, of Kirsty, sitting beside him on the rocks, catching fish, smiling, pointing towards the sea where a white yacht was sailing.

He cleared his throat. "Gran sent you this, you and Jean have to share it between you." He placed a box on the bed filled with little pots of home-made jam, all of them different flavours. Tucked in beside the jam was a sandwich box piled high with crumbly home-baked scones.

"For your tea – in case – in case you get hungry . . ." He stopped, unable to go on.

"Jean, lassie," Mr Anderson said huskily, taking his daughter's hand and holding it tightly, "the house is so strange without you. I miss you out there in the fields with me, I miss hearing you stick up for me when your mother gets on to me for not washing my hands properly . . ."

He could say no more. He couldn't find the words to convey to her all that he was feeling. It was difficult to believe that this was his Jean, the child who had captured his heart from the moment she was born. All through her life she had delighted him; she and he had been friends from the start. As a baby he had held her and had soothed away her tears, as a small child he had comforted her and had helped to still her fears. And later she had comforted him in a thousand different ways. She had always been ready to help on the croft, she had walked with him through the lambing fields, she had worked alongside her brothers, ably and willingly . . . and she had run, as swift, as agile, as a deer; he could see her now, her hair streaming behind her, her smile lighting her face – now here she was, too ill to move from her bed . . .

"Dad," her hand broke free from his and she reached up to touch his face, "I'm with you, I'm with you all. Whenever I feel down I think of Sanda and the croft and you and Mum and the boys and it makes me feel better."

"We'll be here, Jean," her mother said softly, "me, dad and the boys. Just rest now, close your eyes and rest."

"Dad," Kirsty held on to her father's hand. "I'm afraid, Jean is so ill. I think she's going to die soon. That's why all her family are here together, isn't it?"

"Ay, Kirsty." Mr McKinnon spoke honestly, his voice low. "Jean knows, she isn't saying as much but she knows."

Kirsty closed her eyes, her lashes wet. "I wanted so much for her to get well again, I don't know what I'll do without her." Kirsty felt very tired, her eyes were growing heavy, but there was something she had forgotten, something important . . .

"Gran," she whispered. "I forgot to ask. How is she?"

"Improving rapidly." Mrs McKinnon tried to keep her voice steady. The doctor had warned them that Kirsty was reaching a crisis point in her illness and it looked very much as if it wasn't far off. "You know Gran," she continued softly, "as tough as nails, just like her granddaughter."

Jean was feeling weary beyond measure. It had been an exciting afternoon, her parents, her brothers, all there at her bedside, bringing with them a breath of Sanda's clean air. Their voices so lilting, their laughter so dear . . .

She felt her mother's hand on her brow, soothing and relaxing her. She closed her eyes and she slept.

Before Kirsty drifted off she was aware that Hamish was there at her bedside, his young face filled with concern.

"Don't worry, Hamish," she whispered. "I'm going to get well and then I'm going to live in Donside with my family. You and Jean and Robbie and Jim can all come and stay with us at Red Rowans. We can fish in the stream and walk in the hills, all of us together."

Then everybody seemed to go away but there was a warmth in her ear and Andy's voice spoke to her. "Kirsty, I'm sorry, I knew how much you wanted to live at Red Rowans but I didn't want to listen. Say you'll forgive me, say it, Kirsty."

"Of course I forgive you, Andy, you're my brother," she murmured before she felt herself drowning in sleep that she wished would go on for ever.

Andy looked down at her sleeping face and swallowed hard. Taking something from his pocket he placed it on her bedside cabinet. It was one of his favourite photos; it showed Kirsty held high on the shoulders of a group of boys, her arms raised above her head in triumph because she had just saved the game for her team. "You'll win again, Kirsty," Andy whispered softly before turning quickly on his heel to join his parents.

"I'm going to see Gran tonight," he told them.

Mrs McKinnon didn't fail to notice her son's moist eyes. "She'll be delighted, Andy. Give her my love and tell her I must be here beside Kirsty. She'll understand."

Granny Reid was back home in her flat in the sheltered housing complex. She was as bright as she had ever been and twice as determined-looking. She greeted Andy with pleasure and surprise. "My long lost grandson! I was beginning to think you'd forgotten your gran. Such a busy lad these days, always dashing off to music rehearsals or football, yet there was a time when you and me were great pals and you told me all your little problems."

"I know, Gran." He looked uncomfortable.

Her eyes twinkled. "Boys just get a wee bit forgetful o' their folks at your age. You'll change again when you're older. Enough o' us, how's my lass? I hear she's back in hospital."

"It's Kirsty I want to talk to you about!" The words burst out of him, his face red and earnest. "I think she's a bit delirious. When we went to see her this afternoon she spoke in her sleep about Red Rowans. She still thinks we're going to live there."

Granny Reid raised her brows. "And aren't we?"

Andy reddened further. "Mum thinks you wouldn't be fit enough; she and Dad have been talking. They're taking our house off the market. With Kirsty so ill and you just recovering from your heart attack they believe it's the only thing to do . . . And – and even if Kirsty gets better Mum would never go away and leave you here – so we're back to where we started."

"What do you mean, Andy? *If* Kirsty gets better? Of course she's going to get better and we're all going to Red Rowans together. Good God, lad! The thought o' going back to the old place was what kept me going when I was ill! I'm certainly not staying here. If I do I'll be old before my time and will die before my time. No, Red Rowans it is! Kirsty needs to know that her dreams will come true and I need a change in my life before I get too old."

182

Andy's heart was growing lighter by the minute. This was his gran, strong-willed, invincible, a tough old bird.

"But the flat, Gran," he went on, "no one seems interested in buying it and we have to sell it to get money to do up Red Rowans."

"Listen, Andy," Granny Reid lowered her voice to a conspiratorial whisper, "I've got money, your granpa left me comfortable. I've also got the proceeds from my house when I sold it to come here. It will be more than enough to modernise Red Rowans."

"Mum won't hear of it," Andy held his breath.

"She'll hear it and like it. I've had enough o' her tantrums this year. She and your dad can always pay me back when your flat is sold, though when I die – which I don't intend to do for a long time – the money will belong to the family anyway. The important thing at the moment is to get the house ready for Kirsty when she gets better. Oh, and I've been thinking about something else. We'll need a car when we move as your dad had to sell his when he lost his job in Paisley. So the first thing to do is look at cars, and I don't mean just any old banger, I mean a proper motor with all the parts in good working order."

Andy couldn't help himself. Rising, he gave the old lady an almighty bear hug. "Thanks, Gran!" he cried, forgetting to be cool in his excitement. "I want this for Kirsty, more than anything – and you've made it possible."

"You're throttling me to death!" she protested but when he let her go she removed her glasses and wiped her eyes. "I'm glad you've come round to our way o' thinking, lad," she told him with a watery smile. "Now, let me get us a nice cup o' tea then we'll sit down and make lots o' nice cosy wee plans for the future."

Chapter 20

Outside the hospital window the stars were winking in a frosty sky. Kirsty couldn't sleep. She felt sick and heavy, but more than that her heart was sore for Jean who lay so ill in the next bed.

It was quiet and peaceful in the ward. An old lady snored gently in the silence and Jean's erratic breathing seemed hardly to intrude into the dreamings of the night.

In the middle of the ward a tiny glass wind-chime hung from the night-light, glowing with red, green, blue and orange hues.

The colours of the rainbow, thought Kirsty, just like the lovely ones we saw on Sanda. Sanda. She lay back on her pillows, remembering that wonderful holiday, all of them so happy, Jean laughing and running over the fields, playing on the beaches.

Now she was dying and would never run again. Kirsty's eyes blurred. Turning her head she gazed up at the sky, seeing the stars through a veil of tears. One star was bigger and brighter than the rest. Kirsty tried to see it as a symbol of hope.

Her lips moved. "God," she whispered, "Jean is the best friend I ever had, she wanted to do so much with her life, now she'll never see her island again. I hope there will be rainbows in heaven and places as beautiful as Sanda so that she will be happy for all time and never be sick again." The simple prayer made her feel better. There was a stirring from Jean's bed and her voice came faintly.

"Kirsty, are you awake?"

"Yes, I can't sleep."

"Kirsty, can I tell you something? I'm afraid, more afraid than I've ever been in my life, yet I'm so tired I'll be glad in a way when it's over. It gets to be like that – you want to cling on but it becomes too much."

"Oh, Jean," a sob caught in Kirsty's throat, "I love you, you were always the strong one, you still are, even now."

"You're strong too, Kirsty, and I'm so glad we met and became such close friends. It's because we understand one another that I want you to promise me something."

"Anything, Jean, I'd do anything for you."

"I want you to tell me that you won't be sad when I die. Remember all the things that Meg told us. Do all the things you said you would do with your life. Just think of me sometimes, and all the things we shared when we were together."

Kirsty's heart felt as if it were bursting with sorrow. She didn't answer for a moment. Instead she looked up at the enamel rainbow brooch and the little seal stone hanging above her bed. "Every time I look at my seal stone I'll remember you, Jean."

"It brought me luck over the years; it will do the same for you. Somehow I feel that it let me meet you. That was good, wasn't it, Kirsty?"

"Yes, oh, yes, that was good, Jean, the best thing that ever happened to me."

"You haven't promised me yet. I need to hear you saying it."

"I promise," vowed Kirsty shakily.

Jean sunk into her pillows. "Is it cold in the ward, Kirsty?"

Kirsty felt hot and feverish and wanted to throw off the blankets. How could Jean feel cold in such a warm, stuffy place? The answer came suddenly to Kirsty. Jean was cold because her weary body had no more strength left to fight.

The night nurse came up just then to see why the girls were awake. "Please, Nurse," Kirsty said urgently, "would you get my Chinese dressing-gown and wrap it round Jean's shoulders. It reminds her of Sanda, she always admired it."

The nurse took the garment from Kirsty's locker and tucked it round Jean's shoulders. "Does that feel better?" the nurse asked kindly.

"Lots better," Jean said softly. "A cloak of many colours, the turquoise of the sea, the blue of the sky, the crimson of the setting sun . . ."

Her voice trailed away, the nurse looked at her anxiously, then hurried away to get the night doctor.

The next few hours passed in a blur for Kirsty. She drifted in and out of sleep, so ill herself that she was only vaguely aware of the screens round Jean's bed and the doctors and nurses who came and went all night long.

Then the doctors came to her, though she could only see and hear them through a thick, silent fog that swirled in her head. As if in a dream she heard the voices of Jean's parents and brothers, the sound of their sorrow, the last farewells to a beloved daughter.

In her half-conscious state Kirsty knew that her friend had slipped peacefully away in her sleep and strange visions passed through Kirsty's mind. She and Jean were back on Sanda, wearing shorts and shirts because it was summer. The bees were buzzing in the wild thyme, the larks were singing in the blue sky.

She stood with Jean at the door of Croft an Cala, looking out to sea. Shafts of sunlight were lighting the waves, an enormous rainbow appeared in the sky, and suddenly Jean was in the rainbow, part of the brilliant colours, part of the earth and the sea and the sky.

Kirsty wanted to get inside the rainbow too

but Jean wouldn't let her. "Go back, Kirsty," she called. "One day you'll travel beyond the rainbow, but not yet, not yet . . ."

Kirsty stood alone now at the door of Croft an Cala, her hand upraised in farewell to Jean. "Goodbye, Jean," she called. "Someday we'll meet again . . . someday . . ."

Jean had disappeared into a world filled with rainbows, a beautiful world flooded with colour and light and beauty.

Then the visions faded from Kirsty's mind and she was back in the hospital ward, vaguely aware that her mother and father were sitting by her bed, touching her, their eyes filled with love for her . . .

Soon afterwards Kirsty received a bone marrow transplant.

For days she drifted in and out of consciousness. She knew that Andy came to see her. She could hear his voice but she couldn't see his face because her eyes were too heavy to focus properly.

"It's going to be all right, Kirsty," he murmured. "You're going to get well and then we're going to live in Donside, all of us, Gran, Mum and Dad, you and me."

One morning she awoke and this time there was no mist to mar her vision. She could focus her eyes and saw the sun through the window and a little robin pecking the breadcrumbs Nurse Bradley had put out on the sill. A pottery dish filled with dried rose petals was on her locker, reminding her of summer, but it was autumn outside; the trees were turning, the sun was going in behind a watery cloud.

Dr Kominski appeared at the bedside, smiling down at her, his keen eyes studying her face, his fingers on her wrist, taking her pulse. "You're looking much better, young lady," he said in a pleased voice. "You're responding well to treatment. We managed to find a bone marrow donor and although it's too early to be sure, it looks as if it just might be successful." He didn't tell her of the desperate search to find a suitable donor, nor did he say that it had been their last hope of curing her.

Kirsty watched him go, thinking how much she had grown to trust and like him, a man who truly cared for his patients and wanted nothing more than to see them well.

Slowly she recovered. On an October morning of pearly mists and drifting autumn leaves she sat up feeling ravenously hungry. The smell of bacon was wafting through the ward. Nurse Bradley brought a tray laden with cornflakes, bacon and egg, and a little pot of tea.

"I want to see every scrap eaten," said Nurse Bradley, folding her hands over her stomach and beaming down at the girl, so thin and frail, but getting better, oh yes, much better with every minute that passed.

As she ate her breakfast, Kirsty's eyes were once more on the window. A shower of rain was cascading down, followed by rays of sunshine poking through the clouds.

The robin had finished his breakfast of cake crumbs and now stood on the gardener's spade, shaking the raindrops from his wings and making his own tiny rainbows in the process.

There was no stopping Kirsty now. The colour returned to her cheeks, her hair grew in, a cap of shiny brown curls, the kind she had always wanted and which Andy had said might be hers one day.

In her absence from home Red Rowans had been completely renovated. By Christmas the family were ready to move to Donside and when the great day came she sat beside Granny Reid in the back of the new car, Andy and her father in front, her mother having gone on ahead to warm and air the old house.

It was a long picturesque drive to Donside, the bracken was golden on the hills, the rowan berries still clung to the trees. Then at last Red Rowans, a big, sturdy house with lots of windows and gables, sitting snug amidst the hills and glens of Aberdeenshire, smoke puffing busily from the chimneys, Chanter sitting at the door to mew a welcome as Kirsty came up the path.

"Dad will be home every night," Andy told his sister, hardly able to contain his excitement.

"We'll spear fish in the river," Mr McKinnon said, his blue eyes sparkling.

"You and Andy can continue your music in your new school in Aberdeen," Mrs McKinnon added in her practical way.

"Our first Christmas at Red Rowans," Kirsty said in delight.

"And the house cosy with central heating and a nice big fire in the living room," her mother remarked thankfully.

"And maybe a cup o' tea to go with it," put in Granny Reid with asperity. "It's been a long journey and I'm gasping for a cuppy."

At the door Kirsty paused, gazing towards the far-away hills. They rose up against the sky, strong, silent, beautiful. The wind blew down the valley and in the sigh of its voice she seemed to hear Jean calling out to her, telling her to do all the things she wanted to do with her life and not to be sad for her.

"Remember, Kirsty, for ever we will be."

"Yes, Jean," Kirsty whispered, "for ever."

She knew in her heart that she would never forget Jean and the closeness they had shared when all the world was theirs and the sky was filled with rainbows.